TOUGH TIMES

A Novel

MILTON MELTZER

Clarion Books
a Houghton Mifflin Company imprint
215 Park Avenue South, New York, NY 10003
Text copyright © 2007 by Milton Meltzer

The text was set in 12-point Goudy Old Style.

www.clarionbooks.com

Printed in the U.S.A.

Library of Congress Cataloging-in-Publication Data

Meltzer, Milton, 1915–
Tough times / by Milton Meltzer.
p. cm.
Summary: In 1931 Worcester, Massachusetts, Joey Singer, the teenaged son of Jewish
immigrants, suffers with his family through the early part of the Great Depression,
trying to finish high school, working a milk delivery route, marching on Washington,
and eventually even becoming a hobo, all the while trying to figure out how to go to
college and realize his dream of becoming a writer.
ISBN-13: 978-0-618-87445-3
ISBN-10: 0-618-87445-3
[1. Depressions—1929—Juvenile fiction. 2. Depressions—1929—Fiction. 3. Family
life—Massachusetts—Fiction. 4. Massachusetts—History—20th century—Fiction.
5. United States—History—1919–1933—Fiction.] I. Title
PZ7.M5165 Tou 2007
Fic—dc22
2006102765

MP 10 9 8 7 6 5 4 3 2 1

For Ben and Zack,
my tough guys

1

Miss Larkin was reading from Shakespeare, and I was studying the back of Kate Williams's head, when the afternoon gong went off. I liked the way the loose ends of Kate's black hair played on her neck. She turned just then and looked straight at me with those great glowing eyes. But I could hear Miss Larkin's voice go right on, just as if the bell hadn't rung:

"They said they were an-hungry; sighed forth proverbs:
That hunger broke stone walls; that dogs must eat;
That meat was made for mouths; that the gods sent
    not
Corn for the rich men only.

"That's enough for today," she said, closing her book.
With any other teacher, we'd have shot out of our seats as soon as the bell began ringing, or maybe a split second before. You didn't do that in Agnes Larkin's class. Even if a dumbhead like Hank Newton was reciting, you waited for Miss Larkin's signal.

I began pushing up the aisle to the door, where Kate would be waiting for me. But Hank, who sat beside me, was whining. "Why's Aggie drag in this guy Coriolanus, Joey? Ain't we got enough to do learning *Macbeth?*"

"I don't think she's going to make us study the play," I said. "She just hopes someone will want to read Shakespeare even if he's not an assignment."

"She nuts? Why would that stuff about meat and corn make me hit the book?"

"Because," said Kate, who was in the corridor with us, "lots of those old Romans were hungry then, and lots of people are hungry now."

"Well, what's Aggie want us to do?" asked Hank. "Eat poetry?"

I laughed. "Bet you'd rather do that than read it," I said.

Hank reddened. "You a wise guy? The smart aleck always knows the answers!" He reached out to shove me.

Before I could move, Kate caught his arm. "Cut it out," she said. "Can't you take a joke?"

"Tell bigmouth there to stay away from me." And he walked off, a little guy hunched over, his hands stuck deep in the pockets of his mackinaw.

I was shaking.

"You shouldn't have done that, Kate," I said. "I can take care of myself. Now that guy'll go around saying you're my bodyguard."

"Oh, forget it, Joey. He's so frail, if you hit him, he'd break apart."

"That's the trouble. I wouldn't have hit him. I should have, but I probably wouldn't. I'd have tried to argue with him, make him see how stupid that crack was."

"But he's such a miserable kid, Joey. He'll say anything, do anything, just so you know he's there. Do you think socking him or reasoning with him would help?"

"I still wish I'd hit him."

"No you don't. What would you have said to his father?"

She was right. Hank's one thing, but his father—that's something else. I worked for Mr. Newton, riding the milk truck with him every Friday and Saturday night. Mornings, really, for we didn't start till two A.M. I loved getting up in the dark when Grandpa woke me. Once up, I'd put out the light so he'd fall asleep fast. He'd soon be snoring under the blanket, three short snorts of sound followed by one long. I would pull his blanket down so he could breathe better. The moonlight spilled over his head, and I saw how pitted his cheek was and his neck crisscrossed with wrinkles. I wondered how old you had to be for that to happen. It made me feel creepy for a moment. But I knew I'd never live that long.

I'd slip down the two flights of steps to the backyard and out front to where Newt—everyone called him that—was always waiting, his khaki overseas cap cocked over one eye, the tip of his cigarette glowing in the dark behind the windshield.

Newt's milk route was on our side of Worcester, where mostly working people lived. The streets were lined both sides with three-decker tenements built of wood, like the one we lived in. Ma often said she couldn't believe what a bargain these apartments were. Thousands of the three-deckers had been thrown up quickly and filled immediately by the great wave of immigrants like my father flooding into the town, eager for the jobs in factories springing up all over.

We had the top floor, with two bedrooms, a kitchen, a bathroom, and a parlor. Plus a small porch out front and another in the back. The Bass family had the second floor, and the Reeds, who owned the three-decker, lived on the first floor. Not much ground around us, but enough along one side for a few trees and a bit of grass.

I'd hop in beside Newt, and we'd talk till we reached the beginning of our route. Then I'd go around to the back and balance on the tailboard, lean into the truck, grab a metal rack, fill it with bottles, and jump down, taking the customers on one side of the street while he'd take the other side. He was a little slower than me, he was a lot older, and he limped.

One bottle on the first floor for the widow Polasewicz, up the stairs and five bottles for the big Murphy family, up another flight for two milks and the cream that fancy Mrs. Gould had to have. I learned fast what every customer took. Then clattering down the steps, picking up the empties along the way. Back to the truck, stow the empties on one side, load another rack for the next three-decker.

Here and there we'd stop at grocery stores to drop off cases of milk in their doorways. Best part of the night was when we'd both feel hungry (around four, it usually was), and we'd swipe a fresh-baked loaf from the baskets the bakery truck would leave at the grocery and tear off big mouthfuls, washing down the delicious crusts of warm bread with swigs of cold milk from one of the bottles.

It was during one of those breaks that I learned about Newt and the war. We'd picked up the morning paper from the pile dropped in front of Hymie Ruch's candy store before he opened. We were looking at the front page of the morning paper when Newt poked a finger at a headline that read JAPANESE ARMY INVADES MANCHURIA. He grunted, "We'll soon be in that one, too."

"What's that got to do with us?" I said.

"Nothing. No more'n the last one. But just you wait."

He patted his knee. "That's where I got it—shell fragment at Château-Thierry. They put a plate in my knee, but I still don't walk right."

"Gee, Newt, what was it like?"

"Like nothing you'd ever want to see," he said. "Don't be no hero. 'The Yanks are coming,' and I was bound to be one of 'em. Didn't need to. Married, a family started, all that, but I went. . . . What'd I ever get out of it?" He took the overseas cap off and fingered the frayed edges. "Know why I wear this all the time? To remind me of what a jerk I was."

A jerk? Did my father feel like that? He'd been in the same war, but thank God he'd come through it whole, uninjured. Still, he didn't like to talk about it. Once, when he was reading the paper, he slapped it angrily and burst out, "Will they ever pay us that bonus they promised? Congress votes for it, and that sourpuss in the White House, he vetoes it! Just listen to this," and he read aloud what the president said: "'We owe no bonus to able-bodied veterans of the World War.'"

"Yes," Ma had said. "Even if it's only a dollar a day, it'd help. Like Joey's job. Every little bit helps." And she smiled at me.

"I was in the service seventeen months," Pa said. "That would mean about five hundred dollars. It sure would be nice to have in these hard times!"

I knew why Pa had joined up. He was twenty-five then, older than most recruits. But military service would speed up getting his citizenship papers. So he left Ma and me and my sister, Helen, in the care of Grandpa. Helen was five, and I was two. But as the war was winding up, Helen was gone. The flu epidemic. It killed millions worldwide, and somehow it took Helen but missed me. No one ever talked about my sister or about

Pa's time in France. All I could worm out of him was that he was in the infantry, a buck private. Once when I pressed for details, he snorted and said, "Stop looking for a hero, Joey."

It would be almost daylight by the time our truck pulled up again in front of my house. Newt would reach into his pocket, dig out a half dollar, and slip it to me. I'd yell, "So long!" and climb upstairs to my room. Grandpa was almost always up, sitting in the old rocker by our window, looking out over the back piazzas of our neighbors, watching the early sun glide from window to window.

In the beginning I ached all over so badly, I would've quit if the family didn't need the money. Well, if it weren't for Newt, too. I never knew you could feel so tired, arms and legs turned to lead, back sore, fingers stiff. The first few times, I flopped into bed after dawn and slept all through the day, unable to get up even to go see Kate. But gradually my muscles got tougher, and I could swing those bottles through the night, sleep six hours, and be ready for anything.

Kate knew how much I liked working with Hank's father. I couldn't figure out how a man like Newt could have such a punk kid.

"What's the matter with Hank?" I asked Kate. "Either he doesn't open his trap at all, or if he does, out pops something nasty."

She looked thoughtful. "Maybe it's his mother. He never mentions her."

"Neither does Newt, come to think of it. And it's a year we've been working together."

"Haven't you ever been to their house?"

"No. They live just a block from us, but he hasn't asked me over. I'm glad of that. Suppose Hank was there! He'd spoil anything."

"Wonder why Hank doesn't have your job. I should think Newt would want the milk company to pay his own kid, not somebody else's."

"He did have it, Kate. But I think only a short while. I tripped over something in the dark one night, and *crash!* The whole rack of milk hit the ground. Smashed all to pieces. I felt awful. Newt looked mad, but just for a second. Then he laughed. 'Just so long as you don't drop 'em *every* night,' he said, 'the way Hank did. That boy ate up half my pay banging around those bottles. Couldn't afford to keep him on.' It must have been right after that I got the job. I think Ma heard about it in Hymie Ruch's store. She just up and asked Newt if he'd try me out."

"Your mother sounds something special."

I grinned. "She's that, for sure. But I don't know if you'd like her."

"That why you never bring me over? Don't *you* like her?"

I sighed. "I guess I . . . but Ma's hard to take a lot of

the time. Always on your back, do this, do that, do it now, do it right, which always means do it *her* way. Thinks she knows all the answers!"

Kate laughed. "That's just what Hank said about you!"

"Aw, come on, Kate, it isn't the same thing."

"You mean your mother really *does* know all the answers, but you don't?"

"I'll start keeping score on both of us," I said, "and let you know."

2

That talk with Kate got me to thinking about Ma. How come I knew so little about her? How she came to America, what she did here, how she met Pa? I'm going to find out, I told myself, and maybe even write about it. Lots of the kids in our neighborhood had immigrant parents. But none of them ever talked about it. We were all in such a hurry to be "Americans" that we blotted out the past. If what I found out proved to be interesting, maybe our school magazine would run it. I was on the *Argus* staff. I wrote several pieces for it, too. I'd joined the staff because Miss Larkin was the faculty adviser and Kate was on the staff. Gave me the chance to see lots more of both.

So I tried to get Ma talking about the old days. And to my surprise, once I showed I cared, she was more than ready to pour it out.

Like Pa and Grandpa, she told me, she came to America in steerage, alone, crammed belowdecks with about three hundred other immigrants. All she carried from her little town in Austro-Hungary was the dress she wore, a pot, a teakettle, and an embroidered pillowcase she'd made herself. (That was Ma, all right! Elegant whenever possible.) The steerage floor was damp and filthy, and the air smelled awful. The food? "I can't tell you," she said, "it was so terrible. And they gave us just one small cup of water each day. The thirst—you can imagine. A week of that and I thought I must be crazy to be doing this. No bathtub, and eight toilets for all three hundred of us." But she wouldn't give up trying to stay clean, even when it meant standing in line for hours and hours to get to a washbasin.

Finally, after sixteen days at sea, they all spilled into the immigrant receiving station on Ellis Island. "I headed for the Lower East Side," Ma said, "where I knew I'd be among Jews like me. A family took me into their tenement flat. You know—three other boarders squeezed into two rooms. And the cost? Fifty cents a day for bed, breakfast, and supper."

Then, almost as an afterthought, "And Joey? Know who one of those boarders was? Your pa! That's how we met. He was working in a factory making bedsprings. I fell for him pretty fast. . . .

"I got a job in no time. In a garment sweatshop. It was in a tenement right next to where I was living. The boss and his family slept in one bedroom. In the front room and the kitchen were the sewing machines for us operators. Then there were basters and finishers working on the big piles of materials—and old people, too, standing, keeping the irons hot for pressing the finished coats, pants, jackets, and other stuff. . . .

"Thousands of shops like that. And the piece rates we got? So low we had to work fifteen to eighteen hours a day, and often seven days a week, for just enough to stay alive."

Once I'd got Ma started, it was as though a dam had burst. She poured out every little detail of how she'd lived then, and at night I made notes on a pad so as not to forget any of it. I wasn't sure the readers of our school magazine would find it worthwhile. Maybe because most of them, like Kate, had very different family histories. You know, old-time Americans, not raw newcomers like Ma.

When I had the piece in shape—struggling to keep it to about two thousand words, the *Argus* limit—I showed it first to Kate. She said she loved it. "Now I understand a bit better what you've told me about your mom." She had trouble reading my scrawl, but she managed to type it up for me. We didn't own a typewriter. I turned the piece in to Alice McGregor, our student editor. She liked it, too. "But you've not signed your name to it," she said.

"No, I'd rather have it taken more as speaking in general for first-generation Americans. That's why I didn't use my own name."

She hesitated, then said, "All right. We'll print it."

When the next issue of *Argus* came out, there was quite a buzz about the piece. Was it fiction? Or fact? Kate told me it was news to lots of the kids. And the fact that it was unsigned only added to their interest.

3

My handwriting wasn't very neat, and when it came time to do Pa's bills the first of the month, I'd have to be awfully careful so his customers could read them. I worked on the bills in the kitchen, where the light was good. It didn't bother me that Ma and Grandpa were sitting around. Pa had a barter deal with a printer—clean his windows in return for Pa's billheads. They were small square slips of blue paper. Across the top, in black, was printed DAVID SINGER, and below, the address, then WINDOW CLEANING. Under that it said, HOMES, OFFICES, STORES, FACTORIES.

Pa had wanted to print the rates per window, but Ma had said no, let people ask. "Write the figure down, and with our luck," she said, "times will change and you'll be stuck with a low price."

"How can a price be *lower* than fifteen cents?"

Pa hadn't answered. So I put in my two cents. "Times could get worse, Ma. Miss Larkin just the other day said Herbert Hoover isn't doing a damn thing about the Depression. If this were like other civilized countries, she said, the government would do something for people who can't find work."

"I remember," said Grandpa, "how just three years ago, when he was running for president, he said on the radio"—and Grandpa rolled his eyes piously to heaven—"'I promise, with the help of God, to abolish poverty. A chicken in every pot, two cars in every garage, and silk stockings on the legs of every woman in America.' All that, the man promised. And here it is 1931 already, and what do we have? Nothing!"

"At least I'm still working," Pa said.

"And me, too," I had to get in.

"Who said you're not?" said Ma. "But for what? Nothing! How much can fifteen cents a window amount to? An army would have to clean the windows from here to California to make ends meet at that price!"

Pa's face stiffened. He pushed his plate away and left the kitchen. Grandpa stared at Ma. When her eyes met his, he shook his head. "Does it help to make him feel worse?" he said.

Now I flipped through Pa's black record book, where he kept track of the work he'd done, and I made out a bill for each job finished.

Mrs. Mayfield
10 windows @ 15 cents each, $1.50.

That was a big old house. I'd noticed it when I was out walking with Kate. It was on her side of town. How many hours did it take, I wondered, to clean all those windows with their small panes of glass? He used to charge for twenty-four windows, but when Pa had done them the time before, Mrs. Mayfield had announced she was not using the upstairs rooms any longer. Pa was to do only the first floor from then on. Even she felt she had to pinch pennies.

It didn't take long to finish the bills. Each month it took less time. Stores Pa had done for many years had gone out of business. Maybe a third of the offices in the downtown buildings were empty. And a number of people had taken to cleaning their own windows. Worse, just the other day a neatly dressed man had knocked at our back door and asked politely if he could wash our windows in return for a meal. Ma said she had laughed at first, but then got mad and chased the man away.

When I finished stuffing the bills into the envelopes and pasting on the stamps, the phone rang. Ma took the call.

"It's David," she said to Grandpa. "He won't be home for supper. Mr. Dillon wants him to finish his house tonight. Why tonight!" she demanded, as though old Dillon were right there in front of her. "David's been working since four o'clock this morning. Isn't fourteen hours enough? But no, Mr. Dillon's having company this weekend," she said, trying to sound as elegant as a society lady, "and his windows must be cleaned *now!*"

"What can you do, Ruth?" said Grandpa. "David wanted to be his own boss. 'Enough of working for somebody else,' he used to say about that bedspring factory. 'I'm going to run my own business.' So now he does—and he has a hundred bosses."

"But if he'd stayed in that factory," Ma said, "today we wouldn't have a bed to sleep on ourselves. Who buys new beds now? At least windows have to be cleaned."

I wasn't so sure. The windows in my high school were so filthy, you could hardly see the girls passing by on the sidewalk. First the school board had cut down on maintenance, then they'd stopped buying books and supplies, and now there was a rumor that there soon wouldn't be money even for teachers' pay.

"Can I take Pa's supper to him?" I asked. "And mine too, so we can eat together?"

"Of course, Joey. Do some homework while I get things ready."

I left the house toting a brown bag packed with two sandwiches, soup in one thermos, and coffee in another. As I walked through the dark streets, the radio voices of *Amos 'n Andy* followed me from house to house. I passed the big lot where we used to play ball. Spread over it were the ruins of a Tom Thumb miniature golf course. I turned left on Mohawk Street. Down the block I saw the marquee of the Rialto. *Cimarron,* it read, but that was the western playing when the place shut down six months ago. On the corner was Himmel's cafeteria. ALL THE FOOD YOU WANT TO EAT FOR 60 CENTS said the cardboard sign leaning against the dusty artificial fruit. Next door was an empty store, and scribbled in soap on the glass was FOR RENT AT YOUR OWN PRICE.

Past the shopping district were the big houses. Rich families used to live in them, but long ago, before I was born, all of them had moved to the West Side. Their homes were chopped up into small apartments now, and the yards were full of junk.

Beyond, I could see the long granite wall that hid Mr. Dillon's house. It was so high, I couldn't touch the top. All you could see from the street were the crowns of oak and chestnut and elm. I rang the bell at the gate. In a few minutes the gardener, Mr. Testa, came down. He knew me and let me in. I walked up the graveled driveway that curved between the trees and gardens to the front door. Now it didn't seem that far, but when I was carrying full bottles on delivery nights, it felt like a mile. I rang again at the house. I'd never been inside, and I was curious. Outside, it was ugly—cold stone and jagged towers. The kids called it the haunted castle. Mr. Dillon's grandfather had built it when his first factory prospered. Nobody had lived around here then, but the high wall had gone up anyhow. The door opened, and the first butler I'd ever seen, except for Charlie Ruggles in the movies, stood there.

"Yes?"

"I'm Joey Singer. I've brought my father's supper."

"This way," said the man in the rusty black suit. I followed him up a winding staircase to the second floor. Couldn't see what the hall was like, it was so gloomy. At the landing the butler pointed down the corridor and said, "In there, if you please, last door on the left."

The corridor was covered with wallpaper in some dim brown print that looked like cupids dancing in the woods. Next to each door, like sentinels, stood tall heavy chairs. A few portraits of old guys with long beards leaned down from the walls. As I neared the last room I thought I heard voices. I could see the door was slightly ajar. I was about to go in when I heard a strange voice, speaking low and cool:

"You can always do as you choose, Mr. Singer."

Then Pa's voice, hesitant, pleading. "But what choice do I have, Mr. Dillon?"

"Don't make me repeat it again. You can continue to take care of this house on the new terms, or . . ."

I could hear Pa sigh, a deep breath from way down. "Or lose the factory work?"

"Precisely."

Suddenly, I was scared I might be caught eavesdropping. I pushed the door open and walked in.

They were standing by the high windows—Pa with his pail slung over a shoulder, chamois in one hand and squeegee in the other. Mr. Dillon turned at the sound of the squeaking floorboards. He wore a dark blue suit, white shirt, and stiff collar. Old eyes in a stubborn face. As I went toward them, Mr. Dillon began rubbing his forehead with a thin white hand. I noticed the hand trembled.

"It's my Joey, Mr. Dillon. He's brought my supper."

"Yes, I know. Don't be too long with it. The work must be finished tonight."

We sat down as soon as Mr. Dillon left and started on our supper. Pa wasn't saying anything, but then he rarely did. Now and then, as he raised his head to gulp his coffee, he'd glance over at me, and I'd look away. I felt embarrassed. Finally, I said, "Pa, I couldn't help hearing Mr. Dillon. What's he want from you?"

"Not much, Joey. Just that I should do his house for nothing."

"Not much! This place has more windows than Union Station!"

Pa shrugged.

"Why should he expect you to do it for free?"

"I guess you heard. I do it for nothing, or I can forget about his factory."

"The sonofabitch!"

"Well, he's squeezed, so he squeezes me. Everybody knows Dillon Shoes ain't doing so good these days. Your shoe wears out, you keep patching it. You don't buy a new pair."

"Pa—you're making excuses for him. If he wants his house cleaned, then dammit, he ought to pay for it."

"Ought to, ought to, what's ought to? I *got* to do it for nothing, or I don't have his factory to clean."

"But didn't you at least give him an argument? Maybe he'd change his mind."

"Nowadays, Joey, I don't fight with customers."

We finished eating and I stuffed the wax paper and the crumbs into the bag. "Bye, Pa," I said. "See you later."

"You'll be asleep when I get home," he said.

I walked over to the door.

"Oh, Joey," he said. "One thing. You won't mention this to your mother? I'll tell her myself."

I wondered if he would.

4

He did.

And there was one hell of an explosion.

No one was more surprised than me—unless it was Ma.

I'd stayed up later than usual, drinking milk in the kitchen while reading *The Good Earth*, a new novel about China that Aggie Larkin had lent me. When Pa came home—it must have been almost midnight—Ma, who'd been waiting up for him, took one look at him as he walked into the kitchen, and she knew something was wrong. Me, I wouldn't have known. Pa usually has a face I can't read. He doesn't show much expression. People might think he's mad at them because he almost never smiles. I guess it's those two deep vertical lines grooved down his cheeks. They make him look like an old Yankee farmer. I told him that once and got one of his rare grins.

"A Yankee farmer from Bukovina!" he said. Wherever that is.

Anyway, Ma said, "Something's wrong, David?"

"What could be wrong?" Pa said, glancing at me. I shook my head, trying to signal I hadn't told.

"I don't know, David, but something."

"Maybe we could talk about it tomorrow?" He walked heavily to his armchair at the head of the table.

"No, now. I'd like to know now."

So Pa told her. He sort of mumbled the story, acting as if it didn't matter much. But when he came to the part about working for nothing—

"David! You didn't say yes!"

He nodded that he had.

Grandpa came out of our room, pulling his bathrobe tight. He knew the sound of his daughter-in-law's temper.

"But why? Why should you give away hours of your sweat? If you don't have a job, at least you could use the time to rest."

"I told you, Ruth, it isn't just a matter of his house. It's the house *and* the factory. Both, or none."

"I don't like you to take his lip without talking back. At least show that you're a man! Those rich people— they think you're dirt because you do their dirty work. You have to stand up to them!"

"And then what?" put in Grandpa. "Back down and say, I'm sorry, sir, I need the work, forget what I said."

I tried to help. "Don't you see, Ma, Dillon's really giving Pa no choice. What kind of a choice is all or nothing?"

"You keep quiet," she said. "From you I need no advice."

"But the boy's right," said Grandpa. "What can David do? It's eat or don't eat."

Pa, who had said nothing through all this, got up now and walked to their bedroom door. "Ruth," he said, turning around to look at her, "sometimes you act like a fool. Monday *you* get up early, *you* clean all the windows. Then talk." And he shut the door behind him.

I couldn't look at Ma.

Grandpa got up and nudged me toward our room. He lay on his bed, watching me undress. I had only an hour to nap before getting up to deliver the milk. When I was under the covers, he said, "Joey, it upset you, what you heard?"

I nodded.

"It's not so terrible that parents should fight. Better to have it out than hide it. With my Rose, she should rest in peace, I fought all the time."

I never knew Grandma. She died in the old country, before Grandpa came to America.

"But Ma and Pa never fight."

"Not because Ruth doesn't want to. It's because my son, David, he turns away from a fight."

"Pa's not a coward, Grandpa!"

"Who said? When he was a boy, no older than you, Joey, he was the best horse trainer in our district. My father—your great-grandfather—leased some land for a time. There were cows, chickens, cattle, horses. David had a magic hand for horses. He could take the wildest one and gentle it. You should have seen him!" He sighed.

"Pa? Training horses? I didn't know that! He never talks about those times."

"Probably you never asked him. But why should you? It's all a man can do to grow himself up." He rolled over on his other side and went to sleep.

An hour later Grandpa shook me awake. I hadn't needed an alarm clock since he'd moved in with me. He was incredible—could tell himself to wake up at any hour, and presto, he did. I dressed, tiptoed through the kitchen, and passed the other bedroom. I heard scuffling sounds through their door. Were they still fighting? Then I heard the smack of a kiss, and I realized they were making love. I hurried out, feeling funny inside.

5

A week later I had the bad luck to come up against Hank Newton and Mr. Dillon, both in the same day. Kate and I had planned to spend Friday afternoon and evening together, the way we usually did. As soon as school let out, we headed downtown. We thought we'd walk along Main Street to the far end, where the art museum is. Then Hank caught up with us and started talking to Kate as though nothing was wrong. She was nice to him. But I acted like he wasn't there and left him out of the conversation when I had something to say. It wasn't easy to do, but I managed. When we got to Easton's at the corner of Main and Pleasant, we stopped. It had the best soda fountain in town— milk shakes so thick you could chew on them, newspapers and magazines from everywhere, and heaps of junky gadgets and toys all the drugstores had started to sell at "the lowest prices ever."

"Let's go in for a shake," said Kate. "My treat this time."

I knew why she said that. Hank probably didn't have the ten cents. And maybe she wanted to drag out our uncomfortable threesome to see if I'd ever start talking to the jerk.

"Great!" said Hank, of course.

So we went in. There were only two empty seats at the soda fountain. Kate took one, and before I could slide onto the other, Hank had it. We ordered, with me standing behind them—a strawberry for Kate, a mocha for me, and a chocolate for him. While we were sucking on our straws, I happened to look past the fountain and saw Pa cleaning the big plate-glass window opposite. He was working from outside, wearing his old gray pants, faded blue workshirt, and heavy pullover sweater. His cap was jammed down to his eyes to keep the wind from snatching it off. He was totally absorbed in the job, never glancing into the store.

Just then Hank jabbed his elbow back into my gut and inclined his head toward Pa. He'd seen him, too, and wanted me to know it. I started chattering a blue streak to Kate, keeping my eyes away from Pa. When we finished, Kate paid, and we started out. We could have taken the side door, but Hank headed for the front, the door next to the window Pa was still working on. I couldn't do anything but follow. Hank turned left, up Main Street, right past Pa, who had his back to us. I had shut up now, but just as we were going by Pa, Hank said loudly, "Hello, Mr. Singer!" Pa turned around. His eyes took in the three of us. He recognized Hank, had never seen Kate, and knew me, all right.

"Hello," he said, in the kind of tentative voice you use when you aren't sure what's up. Then we were by him, and nobody said anything. At the next corner Hank waved goodbye to Kate and took off.

Two blocks in dead silence.

Then, "So I've met your father at last—thanks to Hank."

I didn't know what to say.

"What's the matter with you, Joey? That *was* your father, wasn't it?"

I kicked an empty cigarette pack that had got in my way.

"He does look like you, a little. I mean, you look a little like him. The same gray-green eyes. Only his have a sweet look. Yours look mean."

Now I'd found a trash basket that needed a good kick to get it off the curb.

"Joey! Aren't you going to say anything?"

"Kate, I didn't see him at first."

"Maybe you didn't—at first. But if Hank did after, certainly you did, too. And you never even said hello!"

I could feel how hot my face was getting. "It's easy for you to act so superior. Your father doesn't have to clean up other people's dirt."

"But he's your father, Joey! You think a man is what he does for a living, only that, and nothing more? He's as good as anybody else!"

"Everybody says so, Kate, but do they really feel that

way? My pa's a window washer; yours is a newspaper columnist. Do people pay them the same respect?"

"Of course they do. Everybody does!"

"They don't. And what's worse, they don't *themselves*. I mean, how can my father feel he's in the same class as your father . . ."

"Go on, Joey, finish it."

"Well, much as I like your father, I'll bet he feels he's better than Pa. Well, bigger, anyway, more important."

"What makes you so sure about your dad? Did you ever ask him?"

"Of course not. I just know, that's all."

Or was it just the way I felt? From the first time I'd been to Kate's house, I hadn't felt at home there. Oh, not that I didn't like being there. Their home was full of books and records, and at the table the talk was about what someone was reading or summers at Cape Cod or seeing a play in Boston. And often what Mr. Williams was writing about.

They were good people, always welcoming to me. But they were so damn sure of themselves. They took it for granted that this was their world, all wrapped up in a gift package. Not that they were rich like old man Dillon. They weren't. "Just plain middle class, like most Americans," the way I once heard Mr. Williams say. Most Americans? I wondered if he knew what little money people on our side of town had. And how it compared with what the *Gazette* paid him.

We were turning in to the museum now, and I was glad to have an excuse to drop all this. The museum's a white marble building, something like the Greek temples Aggie Larkin showed us on slides the time we were reading Homer. There was a whole craze for imitating Greek architecture and naming our cities after theirs, she said, back around a hundred years ago when the Greeks were revolting against the Turks who'd ruled them for about four centuries. Our own revolution was so fresh, she said, we could still get excited about somebody else's. (There was a Greek eating joint in town, the Acropolis, and a movie house called the Olympia, but I'm sure they didn't go back that far.)

Anyhow, the museum wasn't big on Greek art. It had lots of American stuff and European pictures from the Renaissance. Interesting, I guess you'd find it, but for me—and Kate, too, since she's really the one who brought me to it—the best place was the gallery where they had the Impressionists.

Going into that room was like discovering what eyes are for. These artists painted the most joyous pictures, filled with light and color. It was like a guy had been going around with mud on his glasses, and suddenly someone tore them off and let him see the whole shining world. There were none of those battle scenes with heroic warriors that you saw in other rooms, no castles or palaces or nymphs or goddesses. Just natural things— flowers, trees, fields of grain, rivers flowing through meadows, snow and mist and *sun!* And when they painted people, it wasn't lords or ladies, but women at ironing boards, men playing cards, a farmer at work, people dancing, a girl doing her hair. And the colors they used! Not those gloomy browns and blacks, but yellow and orange and violet and blue and crimson and green.

We went into the Impressionist gallery—it must have been the tenth time for the two of us—and I said to Kate how I wished one of these guys would paint the ponds in Elm Park or the Long Meadow in winter when we were skating on it. Or maybe even try those four cypresses the way they looked against the side of our old three-decker.

"What do you mean, 'these *guys*'? How about the women?"

I'd forgotten. Ever since Aggie Larkin had lent Kate *A Room of One's Own,* she was always on the lookout for women who'd done something special. I wouldn't have noticed that some of the pictures we liked were done by Berthe Morisot and an American named Mary Cassatt. We came up to one of my favorites—Van Gogh's painting of a village postman. We stayed back, so our eyes could watch the dabs and patches of color fall into place and the postman spring to life. Then Kate said, casually, "Think Van Gogh would bother to paint a window cleaner?"

I had it coming. She reached for my hand as we walked to the next room.

We were always hoping something new had been added to the collection, though Mr. Williams had said no rich folks would be buying pictures for the museum nowadays.

But there *was* something new. The room, a small one, held only one painting this time. The place was crowded with people. We stood on tiptoe near the door, but it was hard to see the picture over so many heads. "Must be a pretty important picture," Kate said, "to get a room all to itself."

"Let's move closer," I said, sliding into the crowd. It was then that I saw Mr. Dillon standing off to one side. People were pushing up to shake hands with him. I wondered why. Then a photographer raised his camera over the heads in front of him and said, "This way, please, Mr. Dillon!" The old man turned to him, looking solemn but pleased as the flash went off. When we got in close, I could see the painting was a bowl of fruit on a table, and near it a half loaf of bread and a small vase with some flowers. The apples and peaches looked so solid, you could feel their weight in your hand. And their colors were juicy enough to taste.

We bent down to read the brass plate on the frame. "*Still Life*. BY PAUL CÉZANNE. GIFT PURCHASE BY RICHARD DILLON."

Something awful began building in my throat. I was afraid I'd throw up. I headed for Mr. Dillon. He was still shaking hands.

"Mr. Dillon?" I said.

He looked at me. I could tell he didn't remember. "What is it, boy?" he said in a kindly tone, putting out his hand for me to shake.

"You are a crummy bastard!" I said. I could hear my voice coming out loud, but a little shaky.

The people around him drew back, scared; maybe they thought I had a gun or a knife or something. He went dead white, his mouth dropped open, and his hands began to tremble.

I turned around, forgetting about Kate, and started to go. A reporter grabbed my arm at the door and asked, "Who're you?"

"Singer," I said, "Joey Singer. Tell him for me."

Then I ran out of the building, Kate on my heels.

6

It was a long way from the museum to Kate's house, long enough for me to do a lot of explaining. I hadn't told her about the one-sided deal Mr. Dillon had forced on Pa, so she was horrified when I near spit in the old man's face. She thought I'd gone crazy. Now, when she'd heard the story, she understood. "How could that man squeeze pennies out of your father," she said, "and almost on the same day spend thousands for a painting?"

"It's to show off, I bet. Thinks he's the Massachusetts Medici."

Well, I'd fixed him. But suddenly my heart started hammering. What would this do to Pa—to the whole family? Dillon would surely learn who I was, and in one second that'd be the end of the factory job. What would Pa say when he found out? Kate tried to be reassuring. Maybe nobody would tell Dillon my name, or they'd get it wrong, or he'd just dismiss it as kid stuff. She managed to calm me down somewhat. But underneath I was still worried.

Mr. Williams wasn't home for supper that night. He'd been traveling around the state all week to see what was going on in the mill towns. He finally showed up around eight. Wouldn't eat anything, said he didn't feel hungry. He always looked hungry to me. He was a very tall man, and skinny as a broomstick. He was younger than Pa, I knew, but while Pa's hair was still brown, Mr. Williams's was white. He had smoke-blue eyes, a nose that looked like someone or something had broken it, a wide mouth that laughed easily. His voice was rumbly, and though he talked fast, you didn't miss a word. Kate, who sometimes watched him when he worked on columns at home, said he wrote just as fast as he talked.

"How was the trip, Tom?" Mrs. Williams asked. "You're some writer. All you sent were measly post-cards."

"It was awful, Carrie, awful. We don't know the half of it. I thought things were pretty bad here, but the way people are living in those one-industry towns—" He shook his head. "It's one thing to sit in the office and write neat little analyses of economic data, but when you *see* what's happening . . ."

It had been his own idea to take a look. The publisher wasn't happy about it but finally let him go. Pressed for time, he'd stuck to the textile and shoe centers.

Even before Wall Street went smash, the mill workers had lived practically from hand to mouth, he said. But now? Two out of five textile workers were out of work.

Jobless for years, many of them, and those who were working put in only one or two days a week. How could a man support his family, or just himself, on less than ten dollars a week? In the shoe towns it was even worse, he said. Two out of three jobless.

"Know what I found to be the biggest industry in Lowell?" he said. "Charity. Every third or fourth store in that city is vacant. In the tenement districts whole blocks of houses are empty, windows broken, doors smashed, walls caving in, rats running wild. People just up and moved away—where to, who knows? Downtown the only busy store is the five-and-ten. Butchers told me all they sell is tripe and soup bones. Merchants run at a loss, caught in a trap. People owe them so much for years back, they fear if they close shop, they'll never see the debts paid. Yet if they stay open, things may only get worse.

"I talked to doctors. They can't collect their fees. Over half of their patients are charity cases. Dentists told me about all they do is yank teeth out. People can't afford dental care and stay away until it's too painful to go on.

"I never felt so desolate, walking those streets. Shabby men leaning against the brick walls, or standing on street corners, silent men in torn overcoats or sweaters, feet poking out of broken shoes. Sunken eyes in gray faces. Try to talk to them, and they shuffle away."

"How long did you stay there, Dad?"

"Three days was more than I could take. Then I tried Lawrence. The woolen mills are still open, but only for spurts of production now and then. I went there on Sunday and got up before daybreak to watch the mills open. Monday morning hundreds and hundreds of men and women were in the streets, moving toward the mills. But not to work, I found—only to beg for work. They check in every Monday to see if the foreman can promise a day or two of work that week. I learned many have been doing this for months, and some for years. One woman said to me, 'I don't know nothing, only I got no job. No job, no job.' She kept saying it, over and over. After a while I noticed a funny pattern. Men standing around just waiting would do the same thing— clap their hands two or three times, stop, then after a while clap them again. It was a way to act busy. And then the people mumbling to themselves . . ." His voice trailed off.

"What's going to happen, Tom? I'm scared."

"I don't know. In Fall River—maybe the worst place I saw; it's just about dead as a textile center—I talked to a reporter who told me that for several weeks now a group of men, fifteen or twenty, have been going into chain grocery stores and asking for credit. When the clerks says it's cash only, the men say, Move away, we don't want to hurt you, but we've got to eat. Then they fill bags with food and go out. The stores don't call the police. That'd put the story on page one. And the company figures the fewer people who know about it, the better—or other folks would get the same idea. The paper found out what was going on, but it decided not to print the story for the same reason."

"If that kind of thing spreads," I said, "everything will fall apart."

"It *is* falling apart, Joey. Maynard, Housatonic, Haverhill, New Bedford"—ticking them off on his fingers—"they're all disaster areas. And the shoe towns? No better. If anything, the shoe manufacturers are the worst bunch. Always been out for the fastest dollar, the highest profit, and to hell with their workers, the public, or anybody else."

My eyes met Kate's. I knew what we were both thinking. How about here? Was the Dillon factory the same?

"Well, they're not a Johnny-come-lately, like many of the other shoe firms. The Dillon mill's been here for generations. But he's been laying off men who worked in his factory for twenty or twenty-five years. One of those old-timers told me he had practically nothing to fall back on during the layoff. He was half ashamed and half mad. Ashamed because he couldn't take care of his family, mad because he'd let Dillon get away with such low wages all this time, he couldn't put a dime in the bank."

"Are you going to write about it, Dad?"

Mr. Williams got up, walked to the parlor window, stood there looking out at the tall trees arching over the quiet street. "I don't know," he said.

"What do you mean? Wasn't that the purpose of your trip?"

He didn't turn around. "Yes," he said. "But the way I feel—"

"I think we know how you feel, Tom," Mrs. Williams said. "Isn't that what you'd write about?"

"That's just it, Carrie. I'm not sure how I feel. Or rather, what to say about how I feel." He didn't smile. "I'm worn out. I'm going up to bed. How about you?"

"In a minute, Tom. You two know where the icebox is," she said, turning to us. "Help yourselves when the supper wears off. Don't stay up too late, Kate." She smiled at me and followed Mr. Williams upstairs.

It was going on eleven now. If I didn't leave soon, the trolleys wouldn't be running and I'd have to walk miles to get home. There wouldn't be time for a snooze before Newt's truck would be out front. Kate moved over to the sofa, and I sat down beside her.

"I like your father," I said, "your mother—and even *you*." And I started kissing her. She kissed back: slow, tender kisses. Then we were leaning back and pretty soon lying down. The lights were out in the upstairs hall, and it felt like we were in a home of our own. I took out the clasp that held her long hair, and it came down over her shoulders in a silken black wave. I loved to bury my face in its softness. We'd turned off the parlor lights except for a small table lamp in the farthest corner. I could barely see her face in the dark. The whole length of her body was close against mine. I thought I could hear her heart beating in the quiet. I don't know how long we were there, whispering and stroking each other. We'd never done more; I don't know why. It was as though we'd reached a place that we didn't want to go beyond. Not yet. I heard a noise upstairs, and then Mrs. Williams called down, "Joey, you'll miss the last trolley."

I got up, and we headed for the kitchen. As we passed the full-length mirror in the hall, I stopped to take a look at myself. (No mirror this size in our place!) Kate came up behind me, and I saw her viewing me over my shoulder.

"See anything good?" I asked, laughing at her.

"Well, I see a guy we girls call cute." And then, as though reciting in biology class: "Medium height, brown wavy hair, high forehead, nicely shaped face—not too thin, gray-green eyes that change color with changing light, nice straight nose, mouth that breaks into a bright smile, especially when he sees me."

I whipped around and gave her a quick hug. In the kitchen I gulped down a glass of milk, and Kate stuffed an apple in my pocket. We kissed at the door.

I walked to the next corner, where the trolley stopped. The streets were deserted. I looked at the time—the old silver pocket watch Grandpa had given me—and realized that the last car had gone a half hour ago. It was cold. The leaves of the maples were red and yellow on the walks. I jumped into a mound of them that someone had raked together, punted them like a football, and started out. Above, through the half-bare branches, I could see the stars following me home.

7

I got home so late, I hardly had time to get into my overalls before Newt was pulling up in the truck.

It was one of my worst nights on the milk route. I was worried about what had happened yesterday at the museum. Goofus, the collie who slept on the Reeds' back piazza, let out an unexpected growl when I was going up, and I almost dropped a full rack of milk bottles. Then when I cut across the Shermans' yard, jumping the fence the way I always did, my heel hit a picket and an empty flew up in the air. I dove for it and caught it in my arms just before it would have smashed on the sidewalk.

"Nifty catch." It was Newt, who'd watched my performance. "Why're you so nervous tonight, Joey?"

"I'm not," I said. "Just a bit pooped." The truth was, all I could think of was what would be in the morning paper. When we reached the corner of Barclay, the papers had just been dropped at the candy store. I jumped down and tore one out of the bundle. There it was, smack on page 1. Mr. Dillon standing proudly next to the damn Cézanne. My eyes raced down the column under the picture. But not a word about me! I stuck the paper back into the bundle.

That didn't mean old Dillon wouldn't get even through Pa. I waited for the blow to fall. One week passed, then two. Nothing happened. Everything seemed the same. Except that Ma wasn't home anymore when I got back from school. The first couple of days I thought nothing of it. Then I noticed she looked awfully tired when she did come in, around five. That was unusual. Ma had more energy than our whole basketball squad put together.

It was a day or two later that I found out what was up. I'd gone down to the cellar to bank the fire in our furnace before we went to bed. There was a furnace for each tenant. Then, as I was squatting in front of ours, roasting an apple over the coals, watching the skin turn brown and juices bubble, I spotted a kind of small suitcase on a shelf to the side. It was medium blue with white trim, and it looked brand-new. I pulled it down. It didn't feel heavy. But there was something in it. The bag was locked. I shook it. No sound. Then I noticed there were initials stamped in one corner—R.S.

R.S.? Ma's name! Ruth Singer.

I forgot about my apple and ran upstairs with the suitcase. Ma, Pa, and Grandpa were sitting around the kitchen table drinking tea out of tall glasses. I liked to watch the way Grandpa did it. He held a cube of sugar between his teeth and sipped the tea through it.

"Hey! Look what I found near the furnace!" I held up the bag.

"Just put it right back where you got it," Ma said.

"Wait a minute," said Pa. "Did I ever see that before? Looks brand-new to me. You going somewhere, Ruth?"

"Foolish! Where would I be going these days? It's a bag I had to get because it's such a good bargain."

"Bargain or not," said Pa, "where did you get the money for it? Especially when we don't need it?" He'd picked up the bag now and was examining it curiously. He noticed the initials.

"What's this? A bargain? And they throw in gold initials, too? You're getting very fancy, Mrs. Singer."

Then he realized the bag wasn't empty.

"There's something inside," he announced.

"Maybe she's planning to run away," said Grandpa, "and she's packed already."

"What could be inside?" said Ma. "Don't be silly!"

"Enough of secrets," said Pa. "You tell us."

It was plain he meant to know now.

"I was going to tell you," said Ma. "But later, when it would be worked out."

"What's to work out?" Pa asked.

Ma went to her purse and took out a little key. She turned it in the lock, which snapped open. The lid popped up. We all leaned over to look. The suitcase was full of stockings, long filmy ones, all the same color, beige. I couldn't figure out what Ma would be doing with a mess of silk stockings.

I looked at Pa. He reached in a hand and tossed the stockings high into the air. Ma grabbed at them, trying to keep them from falling on the floor. "Are you crazy? What are you doing? You'll get them all dirty!"

"What are *you* doing?" Pa said. "Don't tell me. I know."

He turned to Grandpa and me. And as though Ma weren't right there with us, he said, "She thinks I can't support this family. For her, I'm not enough. *She* has to work, too!"

I didn't get it. "What's this about, Ma? You got a job?"

Before she could answer, Pa was at it again. "Some job!" he snorted. "A peddler! Door-to-door she goes, peddling her stockings, with gold initials on them!"

"Don't be so angry, David," said Grandpa. "What's wrong with peddling? A person needs something, you got it, you bring it to them. So is there something wrong with that? Women wear stockings, and Ruth sells them. Does it hurt somebody?"

"That's not the point," said Pa. "I'm working, I'm paying bills. Ruth has enough to do at home. She doesn't need to be running around the neighborhood, begging people to buy from her."

"But I *do*, David. Any minute winter will be here. We'll need coal. What'll pay the bills? Joey doesn't have a decent suit to his name. What'll buy it? And yourself, how long is it since you've bought a coat to put on your own back?"

"I don't need anything!" said Pa.

"David, please face the facts," said Grandpa. "Maybe I shouldn't talk, I'm such a burden on you already." He put his hand on his right leg, shattered when a crazed mob beat him up in a pogrom. "If I could work, you know I would. But if Ruth can help, why shouldn't she? It's old-fashioned to think women should stay at home!"

"Did I mind when she worked before we had Joey? Didn't we both work then? But *now* is different—now she shouldn't!"

"No, now I *must!*"

"Ruth! I say no! I don't want you climbing those stairs and ringing doorbells and begging people to buy a pair of stockings!"

"I'm not the only one, David. There are women going house to house with corsets and underwear and makeup and God knows what! And it isn't begging, it's selling!"

"To me it's begging. If they want stockings, let them go buy them in a store."

"Then she should get a job in a store, David?" Grandpa was being sly.

"I couldn't get one," said Ma. "I already tried. They're not hiring, they're only firing. All you can get is work on commission. They give you the suitcase, the initials, the stockings, and you go out and find the customers. What you sell, you get a percentage on."

"How much did you sell, Ma?" I asked.

"Enough," she said.

"What's enough?" asked Pa.

"I've only been doing it four afternoons. And I sold a pair, the third afternoon it was. But I'll do better. I need time to learn."

"Four afternoons," said Pa. "That's maybe twelve, sixteen hours of climbing stairs and ringing doorbells. Remember, Ruth, you are no spring chicken anymore. Joey can run up stairs all day, but not you. And if you sold one pair, you made maybe twenty cents?"

Ma bit her lip. "What do you want us to do? The shoe factory you don't have anymore. What will go next? Where will the money come from?"

The shoe factory? Out? The Dillon job dead? When did that happen?

"What does she mean, Pa? You're still doing Dillon's mill, aren't you?"

"No, Joey. Not since last week. That's over."

"But I thought if you did his house for free, you could keep the mill."

"So did I. But a letter came from the plant superintendent. It said they would no longer need my services. I'm out, finished."

"Why didn't somebody tell me?"

"Do I discuss every detail of my business with you? You'd find out soon enough."

"That rotten guy!" I blurted, "I knew he'd get even!"

"What do you mean, get even? For what?" Ma asked.

I'd said too much. Ma and Pa were all over me, demanding to know what had happened. Grandpa tried to hold them off, but I had to tell them. Ma was furious; I thought she'd hit me. But the funny thing was Pa's reaction. I think he was proud of me.

8

Kate's father had holed himself up in his study every night, pounding on his typewriter. When he was through, he had a series of articles about what he called the "tragic towns" of Massachusetts. Kate said he'd taken them to his newspaper—and had them thrown right back in his face. Things were bad enough already, said the publisher. No need to give the gory details. It would only hurt business, and what good would that do anybody?

Kate said her dad was disgusted at first; then he got mad. No one was going to shut him up. If his own paper wouldn't print his articles, maybe someone else would.

So he reworked the series into one long article and mailed it off to *Harper's Magazine*. Two days later the editor phoned. They thought his piece was so important and so powerful that they were ripping out something else to make room for it in the issue about to go to press.

You never saw anybody so excited. Now maybe something would happen!

It sure did.

The article caused a terrific uproar in all the towns he described. The story became front-page news (even his own paper had to mention it) and the subject of many editorials. But most of them were not what he'd expected. No, the editorials denounced the magazine and attacked Mr. Williams. They said if he wasn't a liar, he was certainly a sick man, hard to tell which. City councils passed resolutions against the article, against the magazine, against Kate's father.

Then Kate phoned to give me the news. "Guess what," she said. "Dad's out of a job."

"You joking?" I said.

"No, Joey. The paper fired him last night."

I could tell from her voice she couldn't quite believe it. She was trying it out loud to hear how it sounded.

"I'll be right over," I said.

It was Saturday afternoon. I was just getting up when she called. While I was putting on my pants, I told Grandpa. We were alone; Ma and Pa had gone out. "Him, too?" he said. "A big shot like that they fire?" I'd told Grandpa about Kate. I knew I could trust him not to tell Ma. She still thought I dated different girls, not just one.

When I rang Kate's bell, her father came to the door. "Hello, Joey," he said. He looked the same, except he was in his bathrobe.

I had never seen him like that before. I felt I had to say something. "Mr. Williams," I said, "I heard . . ."

He waved his hand vaguely, as if to say, It's nothing.

Kate came out and we started walking. "How'd it happen?" I asked.

"All those nasty editorials and resolutions were bad enough. But it was the mill owners who did it. They told the publisher he was keeping a Red on the payroll. When Dad heard that, the first time he just laughed. But the publisher didn't. The paper's been in trouble because advertising's fallen off. So when it came time for more layoffs, Dad was on top of the list. He's worked there a lot longer than men who weren't let go. But that didn't matter when they fired him last night. . . . Oh, Joey—what's going to happen to us? I'm scared."

"I bet *Harper's Magazine* would take him on!"

"They won't. I said the same thing, and Dad said they only have a couple of editors and everything else is written by freelancers."

"How's he taking it?"

"Well, last night, when he came home and told us, he made jokes about it at first. 'Maybe the Communists will hire me,' he said. 'I can write their speeches for them.' But by the time I went to bed, he was looking grim. This morning I could hardly get a word out of him. Mom's been telling him he'll get a job on another paper somewhere. But he keeps saying no, he likes it here, he doesn't want to move."

"To move! Gosh, Kate, what'll *we* do?"

"Maybe it won't come to that. Or I can stay here with someone, at least till I finish school."

That didn't make me feel better. I couldn't see her folks moving away and leaving Kate behind.

When we got to Elm Park, we sat down on one of the benches facing the pond. I felt cold and hugged Kate close. Her head rested on my shoulder. We didn't say anything for the longest time. The trees were bare now, and the grass turned brown. The ground felt hard underfoot. I watched two small boys trying to sail paper boats on the pond. A lone duck paddled by slowly, leaving a tiny wake.

"Kate, what are you thinking?"

"Nothing. I don't want to think."

"You won't go away, will you?"

"I wish I could promise you, Joey."

"Promise."

"All right, I promise." She turned her head up, and I bent to kiss her.

"Hey, look at those love bugs!" It was one of the kids by the pond.

We got up and started back to Kate's house.

It was hard to make the time go by. We listened to the radio, tried dancing to a new recording by McKinney's Cotton Pickers, flipped through an album of family pictures—the wedding of Kate's parents, Mr. Williams playing golf, Kate and her mom on a tennis court . . .

Her folks were home, Mrs. Williams with a book in her lap but not really reading it, and Mr. Williams drifting from one room to another. They both seemed sunk deep inside themselves.

Supper was cold cuts and fits and starts of conversation. An hour later I said I'd better go home. I had the milk route to do that night. I thought maybe they'd rather be alone, the three of them. In the hallway Kate kissed me so hard, my teeth hurt.

9

"Tell me, Joey, how's your love life?"

We were sitting around the stove in Margosian's garage, waiting for Newt's milk truck to be fixed. We'd gone over a pothole early that night, and the right rear wheel had almost come off. It was lucky Margosian stayed open all hours.

I grinned at Newt. He knew about Kate—Hank had told him, I'm sure—and he liked to kid me about it. If I just said nothing, it would look like I was very experienced.

"You two planning on going to college?"

"Are you serious? Where would I get the money?"

"What about her?" he said. "Her father had it made."

"I thought so, too. Once upon a time. Till he lost his job at the paper. He's still out of town, looking for another one. And from what Kate says, there aren't any."

"I knew they'd get him for writing that stuff. You don't tell off those mill owners without they hang you for it. Don't tell me—I worked for those bastards."

I hadn't known it. "When was that?" I said.

"Before we came to Worcester. I was raised in Lawrence. Worked in the mills before the war and went back afterward. Those were the good old days, everybody says now. The hell they were. Not for us in those mills. Never could save enough to swap in our old icebox for one of those new refrigerators. Don't even talk about a car! We still had to use a shithouse in the backyard. Somebody was getting rich in those days, but it wasn't us."

"How'd you happen to move here?"

"They shut down our mill. I didn't have a job for two years. Know what the relief people give us for food? Three dollars and ninety-three cents a week. For the whole family! The four of us!"

Four? How could there be four when Hank was the only kid?

He got up, moved over to an old flivver Margosian liked to monkey with, and sat down on the running board. "First I pawned my tools. Then we had to move in with my brother. He has four kids, and he was laid off two weeks later."

He burst out, "People got no right to have kids anymore!"

We lost an hour over that wheel, but we moved faster to make up for it. It must have been going on five when we hit Dillon's place. There was only a field on the opposite side of the street, so Newt sat in the truck while I trotted up the driveway with the cream. I dropped it off at the kitchen door and turned around to go back. It was still dark, and I shivered in my mackinaw. It was close to winter now. I hoped the snow would be late in coming. Ma was pushing me to start wearing my long johns. I'd gone only a few steps back down the drive when I heard a heavy thud. Sounded like something had fallen to the ground from a height. It was behind me, and to my left. I stopped and turned to look.

The big house loomed black against the sky. No lights anywhere. But wasn't one of the windows on the ground floor open? Then I heard rustling in the bushes. I started toward the noise. It stopped. A light went on in the room where the window was open. A man's head appeared silhouetted against the light. The beam of a flashlight shot out from the window, swung across the garden, and passed over my face. I ducked my head, then started moving again toward where I thought the noise had come from.

Suddenly, a figure darted out of the dark and, crouching over, raced toward the stone wall. I tore after it. Whoever it was kept low. He snaked in and out of the trees, leaped over the bushes, pounded across the driveway, and headed for the wall. He reached it with me less than ten yards behind. Now I could see that he was wearing a mackinaw, too. I knew I could catch up before he could claw his way to the top. But my toe rammed into a tree root, and I tumbled to the ground. Just as I scrambled to my feet, I saw him reach the top.

There was the tinkling of broken glass and a muffled scream of pain, and the figure disappeared over the wall. I turned swiftly and headed for the gate. As I broke out onto the street, I saw him scuttling across it. He disappeared into the field on the other side.

I ran to the truck. Newt was slumped over the wheel, dozing. He hadn't seen or heard a thing. I told him what had happened. We went over to the wall. There were fragments of broken glass on the ground. Newt switched on his flashlight, and we examined the wall. Crimson droplets trailed down the stone. "Dillon must have put broken glass all along the top," he said. I wondered how badly the man was hurt.

We went back to the truck and peered through the bars of the gate. No sign of life in the house. The light had gone out.

"Too bad he didn't kidnap the old gent," said Newt.

"That wouldn't have been sensible," I said. "With him the last one in the clan, who else would put up a dime for ransom?"

We laughed.

"I wonder should you tell the cops what you saw," said Newt.

"But what did I see? Never got a look at his face. Still, when I was chasing him, for a second I thought there was something familiar about the way he moved. . . . Anyhow, I'm not going to the police. Let 'em find the guy themselves. It's their job, not mine."

"Maybe he didn't steal anything anyhow. Did you see any loot?"

"It couldn't have been anything much. He was running with his arms free. Unless he had something small, in a pocket."

"Well, forget it," said Newt. "I got enough to worry about without this on my mind. People lose their business, their job, can't pay the milk bill, next thing you know, there'll be no customers for this route." Suddenly, he was gloomy. "I can't go through it again."

I wanted to cheer him up. But it was hard to think of what to say. "How about you being a war vet? Miss Larkin says they should get special treatment from the government."

"She's a good woman, Miss Larkin, only she ain't in the White House. We put in for that promised bonus. But Hoover's against paying it now. We give up a leg, a life, for this country, and he can't give up a dime for us. It's crazy! The papers say the president's lending farmers money to feed their hogs. But not to feed their hungry kids!"

I didn't say anything at home about what had happened at Dillon's. I didn't even tell Kate. Don't know why not. I usually blab everything to her. Maybe it was because she was so worried about her father. She didn't like what his letters were saying. In the last one he said he had a great idea. He'd just read about how fish taken from the Arctic Ocean froze stiff in the air. But when they were tossed into a bucket of warm water, they returned to life. Why couldn't the same be done with him? Someone could stow him away in the bottom of a refrigeration plant and, when things got back to normal again, take him out and throw him into a hot bath. Now, wouldn't that be a workable way of beating the Depression?

That story gave me the willies, too. It sounded like he was about ready to give up. "He'll be all right, Kate," I said. "Only thing is, maybe he'll have to go farther away to find a paper that needs him."

"I wish I could do something," she said. "Get a job so he won't feel so desperate. I'd quit school. But Mom won't hear of it. She's been looking for a job herself and can't find one. Yet she keeps saying things aren't going to be this bad forever. She insists I've got to prepare for college. But what's the use if there won't be any job?"

I couldn't answer that one.

The next day—Monday, it was—we were in Miss Larkin's class, going at *Macbeth* again, Act IV this time. Besides studying the text at home, we read it aloud in class. Aggie made sure we all had a whack at it. She paid no attention to male and female roles but assigned the parts by the seating arrangements. So this time

Alice McGregor happened to be the First Witch, me the Second, and Hank the Third. We stood up in front to read. I liked rolling out the lines:

> "Fillet of a fenny snake,
> In the caldron boil and bake.
> Eye of newt, and toe of frog,
> Wool of bat, and tongue of dog,
> Adder's fork, and blind-worm's sting,
> Lizard's leg, and howlet's wing,
> For a charm of powerful trouble,
> Like a hell-broth boil and bubble."

Then the three of us groaned out the chorus:

> "Double, double toil and trouble;
> Fire burn and caldron bubble."

And now it was Hank's turn. For a mousy guy, he was surprisingly the ham when it came to acting. He seemed to shed his own self and become whatever the part called for. He made a terrific witch:

> "Scale of dragon, tooth of wolf,
> Witch's mummy, maw and gulf
> Of the ravin'd salt-sea shark,
> Root of hemlock, digged i' the dark,
> Liver of blaspheming Jew—"

and right here he turned on me, Witch # 2, and jabbed his finger into my chest, to make sure the whole class knew who the blaspheming Jew was. I would have belted him one if I hadn't noticed that the finger he stuck out at me was wrapped in a dirty bandage. Suddenly, I realized who the figure scuttling over Dillon's wall had been. I was too excited to hear the rest of his speech, and I could barely get through my own lines. By the time we finished the scene, class was over.

I grabbed Kate, and we went into the *Argus* office to make up the school magazine.

"Some control, Joey," she said. "I thought you were going to pop him for sure this time. What happened? You looked sort of dazed."

I filled her in on the crime at Dillon's while we lined up the copy and artwork for the next issue, deciding on what would go where, and who would write the headlines and captions. I held back on my revelation till the very end. . . . "So when I saw that bandage on Hank, I knew he was the guy I'd been chasing in the dark. The mackinaw, the way he ran, the broken glass, the cut finger, it all adds up. Only thing I don't know is what he took, and why."

"Gee, Joey, what will his father say?"

"But he doesn't know!"

"He will, though. Aren't you going to speak up?"

"Me? Why should I? I couldn't care less what's swiped from Dillon. It's up to the cops."

She shook her head. "I don't know—I feel funny about it. Someone's done something wrong, you know who did it, and you don't say anything. Is that right?"

Was it? I was no lawyer, but I'd heard if you saw a crime committed and didn't disclose what you knew, they considered you an accessory to the crime. "But I don't want to be a squealer," I said.

"That's kid stuff, Joey. If every witness to a crime kept quiet about it, no guilty person would ever be punished."

"But I couldn't prove anything. A guy could cut his finger for a dozen different reasons. I never saw the face. And there's more than one plaid mackinaw in this town."

"Yours, for instance," said Kate.

"Yeah, mine. I deliver milk and crack safes. That's my job—Friday and Saturday nights."

"Funny," she said, "very funny."

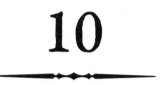

10

How funny it was I found out when I got home that night.

"Joey! What's going on? You're in bad trouble!" Ma said.

"What'd I do now?"

"The police think you stole from Mr. Dillon! They were here for an hour—they just left."

"Two Cossacks," said Grandpa. "A big one and a small one. They took out a piece of paper, stuck it under my nose, and then turned our room upside down looking for God knows what."

I ran into the bedroom. The three drawers of my bureau were pulled open and my stuff heaped on the floor. They'd torn apart my bed and Grandpa's. My closet, too, was wide open, and I could see they'd rummaged through everything hanging up as well as the junk on the shelf.

"They picked up all your books," Ma said, "looked behind them, under them, into them!"

"What did they find?" I asked.

"Nothing! Absolutely nothing! Just like I told them!" said Grandpa triumphantly. "Our Joey is no crook, I said to them. A Rockefeller he is not, but he does not steal. What little this family has, I said, it earns by hard labor. You should go look in Mr. Dillon's palace, I said, and see what a boss steals from his workers. The fancy clothes on his back, the pretty automobiles in his garage, the rich foods in his pantry, the plush furniture in his parlor—everything he has is stolen from our sweat!"

He would have gone on, but Ma interrupted him. "Your speeches they don't want," she said. "What they want is what they say Joey stole."

"That," said Grandpa, "they couldn't find here, or anywhere."

"Believe me, Joey," said Ma, "if I didn't know you, I would have had a heart attack. I tried to tell those men my son couldn't do something like this, but they wouldn't listen. All we know, they said, is that the butler saw your face from the window and then saw you running off."

"Did they say what was stolen?"

"No, that they wouldn't say. Just that they were sure they'd find it here."

"And when they didn't, I laughed right in their face!" said Grandpa.

"And what did you get for it? They searched you, too!"

"Right down to my skin," sad Grandpa happily. "I

even told them to look in my bellybutton for the crown jewels."

Now Ma was smiling. "You should have seen him, Joey. He stands there in his long johns, unbuttons the front, picks the lint nicely out of his bellybutton, and invites them to have a look. Then he turns around, drops the back flap, and invites them to have another look!"

I couldn't help laughing. But I was scared all the same. And one thing puzzled me. "Why didn't the cops stay to arrest me, Ma? If they're so sure I did it?"

"I thought they would. But all they said when they left was that if you had any brains, you'd return what you took, fast!"

"Maybe," said Grandpa, "His Majesty doesn't care about who, only what. He wants back whatever he lost."

"So what am I supposed to do?" I said. "I haven't got whatever it is. Only the thief has. And he hasn't been caught yet."

I wasn't about to say I was pretty sure who the thief was. They'd try to make me tell the police.

When Pa came in, he got the whole story from Ma and Grandpa. It didn't help his supper go down. He sat there slowly chewing his food, looking at me while listening to them. I had a bad feeling. When Grandpa finished his tale of how he'd made fools of the Cossacks, Pa said, "Well, Joey?"

"Well what, Pa?"

"Did you do it?"

"For God's sake, Pa!"

"What are you saying, David? You don't believe Joey stole!"

"I'm only asking."

"But you shouldn't even ask!" Grandpa said.

"Some people steal, some people don't. Today, more do. They're hungry, they're sick in the head, they don't care anymore what's right and what's wrong. I know."

"You know what, David?" Ma asked.

"I myself, I stole."

I didn't think I heard him right. I looked at Ma. Her mouth dropped open, then she smiled an unbelieving smile.

"This is no time for joking," said Grandpa.

"Ruth, you remember once, long ago, I told you how when I was working upstairs in Mrs. Mayfield's, I heard her below calling to her daughter, 'Lock that drawer— the window cleaner will be down soon.' Well, the last time I was over there, I was doing a window in her husband's den and I saw rolls of stamps on his desk. I just reached out and put one of the rolls in my pocket. I thought, 'What are you doing?' Then I told myself I need the stamps more than he does. He can buy all he wants."

He turned to me. "Those were some of the stamps I gave you to use when you made out the bills last month."

No one said anything.

"I don't know what got into me, I never did anything like that before. A lousy bunch of two-cent stamps."

Ma began crying. He reached over and stroked her hair. "Don't, Ruth." Then he looked at me. "That's why I asked you, Joey."

"I didn't do it, Pa. Do you believe me?"

"I do. But how will you make *them* believe it? They say someone saw you there that night, running away. Newton can't help you. He was sitting in the truck outside. They'll say you had more than one reason to do it. Not only the value of whatever is missing. But to get even with Dillon because he took away my work."

I hadn't thought about it that way. How could I clear myself? Only by proving that someone else had done it. I decided I'd watch Hank to see if I could find some clue to what he'd stolen. Of course, what I'd do about it if I did find out, I hadn't any idea.

The next day I looked for him in school. Only he wasn't there. Nor the next day, nor the next. Maybe he'd run away? Kate didn't think so; I was sure he had. We argued over it while I was walking her home Friday afternoon. It was early December, and the first snow of winter had started during noon recess. The flakes, fat and lazy, drifted silently down. By now there was enough on the ground for our footprints to show. I began taking huge steps, and Kate behind me tried to leap into my marks so it would look like a giant had come this way. Then we saw the afternoon's headlines on a newsstand:

FIRST NATIONAL BANK COLLAPSES
DEPOSITS LOST

"Pretty soon there'll be more of them closed than open," I said. "Hundreds have already shut down around the country."

Kate looked sick.

"What's the matter?" I asked.

"The First National—that's ours. Dad has his savings there."

We ran all the way to her house, skidding and slipping in the snow. We found Kate's mother in the kitchen, sitting at the table. She still had on her hat and coat. Her hands were clasped around a mug of coffee that had gone cold. She didn't look up when we burst in.

"The bank," she said. "They closed it." Her voice was low, dull, as though she were mumbling in her sleep. "No warning, nothing. I went down there. People all over the sidewalk, fighting to reach the door. It was closed, only a small notice on it. Closed. For good. Our savings gone—all gone."

For a second I felt relieved, because we didn't have money in the First National. Or any other bank. Pa never made enough to salt any away. So we had nothing to lose. But it was terrible for Kate's folks. They'd been living off their savings since her father had lost his job.

"Never thought First National would close," Mrs. Williams kept saying. "Never, never. It's one of the oldest banks. It was like having your money in the United States Treasury. The worst thing was old Mrs. Jackson. She hammered with her fists on the door, screaming and sobbing. When they quieted her down a little, she said she had twelve hundred dollars in a savings account from her husband's insurance and five hundred dollars more she had saved from making rag rugs. Ten years of making rag rugs—and nothing left now but charity." She whispered the last words, as though to herself.

She stood up, went to the stove to pour us some coffee. "What will I tell Tom?" she said. "What will I tell Tom?"

"It's not your fault, Mom."

"I know, but what will it do to him? Oh, I wish he were here! Even without a job, better to be at home than out there in those strange towns!"

"Give him time, Mom," Kate said. "You know he'd hate to be sitting here if it meant doing nothing. At least he's keeping busy hunting for work."

"But how will he go on, with our savings gone?"

It went that way for hours. They'd think it was better not to write Mr. Williams about the bank closing, then

69

no, better to tell him the truth because he'd read about it in the papers anyhow. And besides, there'd be no money to send him each week, and he'd have to know why. But if they could borrow from friends, maybe he needn't know after all. At least for a while.

So they got out pencil and paper and tried to draw up a list of friends. But this one had already lost his job, too, and that one had just taken a fierce salary cut, and another one had many of his own relatives in trouble, and still another was notoriously tight when it came to money. It ended when Mrs. Williams said she couldn't see how they could ask help of any of their friends. The only hope was to write to her brother. He had a good job in St. Louis, where he was manager of a department store. Maybe he could make them a small loan—until there was a job again and they could pay it back.

Mrs. Williams thought of something. "What about your mother's work, Joey?" she said. "Couldn't I do the same thing?"

"If you could find any customers," I said. "Ma's given up."

It was hard to work up their spirits, and I wasn't much help. Kate begged to quit school so she could hunt for work, but her mother still wouldn't hear of it. Instead, she'd try harder to find a job herself. I didn't see how she could try any harder than she already had.

11

The snow was still coming down when I left Kate, so I put out a nickel for the trolley instead of making the long hike home. When I came in, Ma hollered at me for not wiping my shoes dry. The house was shining clean, the way it usually was, but especially on Friday nights.

Ma spent half the day on her hands and knees scrubbing the floors down till you could just about see your face in the bleached wood. I helped by dusting every stick of furniture in the house and then running the carpet sweeper over the parlor rug. In the beginning I squawked—was that a man's job? But Ma said, "Boy or girl, you got to help. What's this nonsense about cleaning being a woman's job? It's how your pa makes a living, isn't it? So get busy!"

I told Ma we ought to sell the overstuffed furniture and the rug and close the parlor. Who ever used it? We did all our living in the kitchen. But she was too proud of it. The only time anyone went in there was when Pa wanted to listen to the radio. We had a Silvertone Marshall in a walnut veneer that must have cost him a lot of windows way back. I guess it was worth it, because he loved the Jack Benny and Eddie Cantor shows. Those were the only times he laughed.

The rest of Friday went into baking and cooking. Ma made a challah that melted on the tongue, and her apple pie and coffee cake "you couldn't get at the Waldorf-Astoria," Pa always told her. As though he'd ever been there. Her cooking was just as great, he said, even though Friday-night supper was always chicken. It tasted just as good the millionth time. By now we weren't eating as much the rest of the week, but somehow Ma kept Friday night—the Sabbath meal—the way it had always been. Not that we made anything religious of it. Pa didn't bother with that stuff. Maybe he didn't care because Grandpa was an old radical, proud to be called an atheist. Pa never went that far, but his faith was certainly watery. As for Ma, she did what Pa wanted—at least in this!—and so I hadn't even been bar mitzvahed.

Still, I think if we'd lived in a different kind of neighborhood, I would have been. This was a very mixed part of town, a lot of Catholic families, some Protestant, and a small number of Jews. What the neighbors would think always mattered to Ma, but since most of them weren't Jews, that was that. Though sometimes this worked out in odd ways. Our family never went to synagogue on the High Holy Days. But Ma insisted on keeping me home from school, because she felt the Gentile neighbors would wonder what kind of people we were if we didn't observe our own religious days. I yelled, "You're a hypocrite!" and Pa smacked me for it. "Show some respect for your mother," he said.

That had been before Grandpa came to live with us. I bet *he* would have backed me up. He was a tough old man. I don't mean big—he was even shorter than Pa, maybe five foot three. It amused him that now, at sixteen, I was a head taller than both of them. "That's America for you," he'd say, "one generation of enough to eat and they're giants already. In the old country we didn't eat so well."

I remember once I took him to the movies on a Saturday afternoon to see an old picture—Charlie Chaplin in *The Gold Rush*. There was that wonderful scene where Charlie's starving in the Klondike, and he cooks and eats his shoelaces as though they were the most delicious spaghetti. We nearly died laughing. Afterward we sat on a bench in the twilight before heading home and reminded each other of the great things in the picture. When we came to the shoelace spaghetti, Grandpa said, "I know I laughed, but a joke it isn't. Poor isn't funny when there's not enough to eat. Often we didn't have bread in the house. We had to borrow a slice, or buy a loaf on credit. Imagine, sometimes not a match in the house to kindle the stove or light the lamp—*if* there was wood in the stove or kerosene in the lamp. . . ."

In his village, he said, they ate mostly potatoes and herring, and when herring wasn't possible, they lived on bread and potatoes. For the big day, Friday, there might be a soup of meat and bones. "We didn't starve," he said, "but we danced on the edge."

From America had come letters saying such poverty wasn't even thinkable in the land of plenty. "Maybe not then," Grandpa said, "but now?" As we walked home, his eyes took in the shabby brick and stone buildings along Front Street, the people drifting by the shop windows, the patchy grass between the scattered trees in the park behind City Hall. "Even so," he said, "I miss it." I knew he was thinking of the old country. "Our place was only a little village," he said, "just a dot on the land. In the summer the wheat, rye, barley, oats— they were like the ocean, so far the fields stretched. In winter an ocean of snow, with the black ice of the rivers cutting through it."

I wondered aloud how come, if there was rich land and grain and herds of cattle and sheep and horses, people could be so poor. "You think it was for us, all this?" he said. "No, it went into the pockets of the landlords, the noblemen, the police—those grafters! It was a hard struggle just to stay alive. Ask me how we managed and I couldn't tell you. If we all sat down to eat at once in our house, we didn't have enough wooden spoons to go around." Then he smiled. "It was like Sholem Aleichem says, 'We were, with God's help, poor people.'"

I had trouble that night getting some sleep in before work. I tossed about in bed so much that Grandpa wanted to know what ailed me. I told him I couldn't sleep because of the mess Kate's family was in, with all their savings gone down the drain.

"If only people would do something!" he said. "It's two years already since the roof fell in. And only now are they beginning to stir! In the *Forward* I read people marched around the White House last week and yelled they're hungry. Do you think he heard? Herbie Hoover? Him with his celluloid collar so high it covers his ears?"

Grandpa got his education from the weekend edition of the *Jewish Daily Forward*, a Yiddish paper that preached socialism. He was disgusted with Pa, who preferred the *Boston American* on Sundays. It was full of features about gruesome murders and sensational discoveries in Egyptian tombs. One Sunday, Grandpa had had enough of it. "Why don't you read a *good* paper?" he demanded. "A paper that tells the truth! This other stuff is garbage. That millionaire Hearst wants you to know from nothing. It makes you feel good to be ignorant?"

When Pa wouldn't argue, Grandpa got mad. "You know something? You won't read the *Forward* because it's in Yiddish. And you and Ruth are so damn much in a hurry to be American, you want to forget your own language! Who ever heard of Jews not talking Yiddish even in their own home! It's a shame Joey's growing up and doesn't know from where he comes!"

Pa squirmed silently behind his paper. But Ma wouldn't take it. "Pop," she said, "you raised your children *your* way, we'll raise Joey *our* way. Not another word!"

That ended the debate before it began.

I must have been asleep only a few minutes that night when Grandpa shook me. "Think you can make it in this weather?" he said, lifting the curtain so I could look outside. The snow was still sifting down. In some places it had drifted almost to the top of our picket fence. "Sure," I said. "Newt'll have chains on the tires, and I can wear my overshoes."

I was pretty groggy when we started out, but the cold air pinched me awake. Slogging through the snow slowed us down. The milk bottles were slippery wet, and I had to grip hard to keep from losing any. Newt drove hunched over the wheel, squinting through the snow that sloshed out of the blackness at our windshield. When we took our break, I snatched up a bread from in front of the grocery and jumped back into the truck so we could be warm while we ate.

Newt looked worn out. He sat there saying nothing, just rubbing his bum knee in between swigs of milk.

I worked around to asking him about what was on my mind. "How's Hank? Don't see him in school these days."

"Not so good," said Newt. "His hand's in bad shape."

I pretended I didn't know. "What's the matter with it?"

"It's all swollen up. He says it's nothing but a little cut. From a can opener slipping. And he won't go to a doctor. I make him soak it in water and Epsom salts. But the swelling hasn't gone down much. It must be infected. If the damn thing doesn't get better this weekend, I'll drag that kid to the clinic if I have to tie him up. Besides, I don't like him missing all this school."

"Gee, I hope he's all right." I could see Newt didn't connect Hank's hand with the broken glass on top of Dillon's wall.

"He better be. I haven't got time to nurse him." Then, as though seeing what was going through my head, "You hear any more from those cops about the Dillon thing?"

"No, but I got a feeling I will. They're not going to sit around forever, waiting for the big mystery to solve itself."

"You can count on me, Joey. I was with you that night. You didn't do anything wrong."

"But they won't care about what you didn't see. After all, you were in the truck when I was on the other side of the wall."

"Hey, you talk like Mr. District Attorney. Prosecuting your own self!"

"No use kidding about it. That's how they'll look at it."

"Ain't you worried?"

Of course I was. But he didn't know exactly why. I had to get myself out of this jam without getting Hank into it.

"If it gets too hot," I said, "maybe I'll disappear."

"Not you," he said. "I can see Hank doing something like that, but not Joey Singer."

"Why not?" I said, feeling put down. "Think I haven't got the guts?"

"It ain't that. I just don't see you running away. I figure Joey's a smart kid, he'll come up with the answers."

But what if I didn't?

"Maybe I can borrow the truck," I said, "and take off in it."

He grinned. "Me first—I got first claim."

"Why? You going someplace?"

Now he was dead serious. "You read about those people come to Washington maybe a week, ten days ago?"

"You mean the Hunger Marchers? My grandpa, he told me about it."

"Well, they got hold of a good idea. Didn't get nowhere—I admit it. But it's a start. And we're gonna do it, too. Only lots more of us."

I was puzzled. "Who's we? Who do you mean?"

He yanked off his dirty old service cap. "That's who," he said, slapping it on his knee. "The vets!"

"Just what are you going to do?"

"It's started already," he said. "We're getting together,

talking it up. We're gonna get the bonus money they promised us, or else!"

"Or else what?"

"Never you mind or-else-what. The way we'll do it, there won't be no or-else."

"But what are you going to do?"

"We're gonna get us all together, the vets, from every which where. And we're gonna march on Washington. When old Hoover and those buggers in Congress see us coming, wow! They'll be shivering in their pants!"

It was the first time I'd ever seen Newt that excited. His eyes were hot, his voice rising. He put his cap on again and tipped it down over one eye. He sure was feeling good.

"Joey, what about your pop? Think he'd join us?"

It hadn't occurred to me. Pa never said anything about his time in the war. But if the veterans could get that bonus, why not him? We sure could use it!

12

That first snow lasted a long time. Now and then a fresh fall renewed it, bandaging over the dirty patches and the bare spots. I went out on the milk route no matter what the weather. But Pa, he was up at one thirty A.M. six days a week to walk a mile and a half downtown and take care of washing the windows of the Sterling cafeterias. If it weren't for that steady job, God knows what we would have done that winter. He had to finish cleaning them all by six A.M., when they opened for business. Their meals were about the cheapest you could get, which I guess is why the cafeterias didn't close down like so many other eating places.

The bad weather etched Pa's skin like acid. His face was wrinkled leather, and his hands were almost black. His fingers and palms were crisscrossed with gashes made by broken glass, constant wetness, and freezing cold. I remember a long time back when I was a little kid and he reached over and stroked my cheek, and I realized how strange his touch was.

Before things got this bad, Pa used to get home in the

late afternoon. Now, with so little work, he'd usually come in from the Sterling job and flop into bed before I got up for school. And when I returned, I'd find him asleep again. In between, Ma said, he'd be puttering around, trying to help her with the housework or sitting over the newspaper. Once, when I stayed home with a cold, I asked him what was new and discovered he wasn't really looking at the paper. He didn't know what was in it; he just held it to feel he was doing something. Sitting with empty hands for long stretches of time seemed to embarrass him. Grandpa played chess and tried to teach Pa how. But Pa couldn't concentrate.

"What's the matter with you?" Grandpa said, getting impatient. "You act like without a full day's work you're nothing. You've given three lifetimes to work already! Is it wrong to use this chance for a little pleasure? Come on, let me teach you!"

But Pa waved him off.

Home from school one afternoon, I picked up the *Gazette*, and there on page 1 was a story about war veterans trying to pull together the biggest possible army for their march on Washington.

I showed the story to Ma. "What about it, Ma? How come Pa seems to be paying no attention to what's happening? Newt's been talking about it at work. He's thinking he ought to join up with those guys."

She was silent for a while. Then: "Joey, I don't know

how to tell you. Those long months in France were a horror for your father. When he came home after the war ended, he was a changed man. It hurt terribly to see him so down, so silent, so unable to tell me what the matter was, what went so wrong. Of course I knew he'd been at the front, and in war monstrous things happen. What could I do to draw him out? To share with me what he'd gone through?"

She told me that years had gone by, until in the middle of one night, in bed, Ma sensed he hadn't been sleeping, and hugging him close, she managed to draw him out. "Only a little at first," she said, "and then, bit by bit, more. I had to patch it together. It was horror after horror." Tears came, and she turned her head away to hide them from me. "I loved him so much, but it was as though he had come home a stranger."

Poorly trained, because they were rushed overseas to help the French and British resist the Germans at a critical stage late in the war, Pa's outfit had gone into action in the Argonne Forest. It was bristling with German artillery and heavy machine guns. On the first day Pa's unit lost about 40 percent of both officers and men. Soon they were near collapse, weakened by diarrhea and fever and the ever-present lice.

"Then, another night, he turned in bed and said to me, 'You want to know? All of it?' And he said, in a cold, almost mechanical voice, 'Bodies decapitated, guts spilled, joints shattered, eyes put out, jaws shot away, hands, feet, arms, legs blown off, littered on the ground, men blistered and blinded by gas. And the noise, the noise! Rifles, machine guns, grenades, bombs, artillery, rockets—all blasting away at once, till you felt that silence, quiet, would never come again.'"

I put my arms around Ma and hugged her close. It was the first time I'd ever done that. After a while the tears stopped. She told me that by some miracle Pa was not wounded in those remaining weeks of the war. "He must have suffered shell shock. Our doctor told me it's a kind of hysteria and anxiety that grabs soldiers in combat. Be patient with him, he said; it can last for a long, long time.

"You were a very little kid when he lost the happy, joyous spirit he once had." All I could remember were the long periods of almost complete silence.

I wanted to let Pa know I sensed what he'd gone through. I wanted to get him to talk, to open up with me. But how? When? Right now the only thing he'd talk about was the Dillon business. Every few days he'd ask Ma if the cops had been around again. And then he'd look at me in a funny way, as if he were seeing me behind prison bars.

"Forget it, Pa," I'd say. "Nobody's after me."

And he'd say, "They're not, huh?" He could imagine them sniffing like bloodhounds at my heels.

Meanwhile, Hank had come back to school, his fin-ger naked to the world, healed so far as anyone could see. Newt told me he'd dragged Hank to the clinic, where an intern had lanced the infection and let the pus out.

My curiosity about what Hank had swiped from Dillon grew almost by the day. There was no sign that whatever it was had made Hank any richer. He had no more nickels or dimes to spend than the rest of us, and that was damn few.

The day when Kate could pay for Hank or anyone else was long gone. Her mother had a job now—if you could call it a job when you don't get paid. She was working, serving food in the Women's Club, where they let her take home the food that had passed its salable prime. There was some of that nearly every day—stale bread, vegetables, fruits—and it helped. So did the few dollars a week that had begun coming in from Kate's father.

Mr. Williams had gotten work in Chicago. At first he didn't say what he was doing. But after they begged him to come home at least for a weekend so they could see him again, he wrote that he couldn't because he was working every day. He had gotten a job as night janitor in a big apartment house. He worked thirteen-hour shifts, seven nights a week. He was sure of the job only till the end of winter. After that, he'd see.

When Kate read me parts from his letter, I thought she'd bust out crying before she finished. But she didn't. She thought her father was something special. He hadn't quit—that was the idea. She tucked the letter back into her jacket pocket. We'd been huddled over a fire we'd built on the edge of Long Meadow. Feeling warm again, we got up and skated out onto the ice. It was a huge marshland, which froze over in real cold weather and made great skating. There was a crackling sound as the ice settled under our weight. Sometimes we passed over places where the water had run out beneath the ice, and a hollow sound rumbled up. Going around a bend, we ran into a thin layer of snow atop the ice. We stroked over it, our skates making a muffled sound, as though we were on wooden runners. Then, suddenly, we were on a surface ridged like a washboard, and catching a snag, I let go of Kate's hand and went sprawling. She stopped and knelt beside me, and when she saw I was laughing, she picked up some snow and rubbed it over my cheeks. I pushed aside the scarf wrapped over her head and, holding her face between my mittens, kissed the snow fringing her eyelashes, then her cold nose, then her warm mouth.

"Joey," she whispered.

"No need to whisper," I said. "Nobody's here but us."

She stood up then, cupped her hands like a megaphone around her mouth, and yelled, "Joeeee!"

"It's me, O Lord," I said, looking up from the ice, "standing in the need of love."

Laughing, she reached down and yanked me to my feet. Now the meadow was making a belching sound, as though the water beneath were heaving up against the ice. We began racing to the far end, Kate a little ahead, sweeping along with a lovely floating motion, leaning now to this side, then to that. She turned with the curve of the meadow, and we skated swiftly in a great arc back to where our fire had almost died out. We clumped off the ice and found some dry leaves and branches to revive the flames. The leaves flashed up like powder, but then the fire took hold of the solid wood and began to devour it. We sat on the white trunk of a birch that had fallen over and watched the flames.

A light wind had come up, blowing snow down from the trees in fine showers. When Kate took off her scarf, her black hair shone with beautiful star-shaped crystals of snow. Above her head red alder catkins dangled at the ends of twigs. It made me think of spring. A long way off.

Kate reached into a pocket and took out a winter apple. I split it in half with the pressure of my thumbs, and we munched its pulpy whiteness.

"Joey," she said, "when'll this be over?"

I knew what she meant. "Think I'm a prophet? That's one question I don't have the answer for."

"But we've so little time to finish school."

"What's that got to do with it?"

"Nothing, I guess. But I always thought when I was through with high school, it would be a big beginning."

"Or a big ending."

"That, too. It's the same thing, really."

"What did you want to be when you were little, Kate?"

"A teacher. At least, that's the first thing I remember."

"How come a teacher?"

"In grade school I had one teacher who was so mean, I used to tell myself I'd be a teacher when I grew up so other little kids could have a nice one."

"But that's not what you want now? Even after Aggie Larkin?"

"No. A writer, maybe. . . . Oh, what's the use of wanting to be anything? It only comes to nothing. When I think of Dad . . ." She reached over and picked a burning twig from the fire. She held it up and watched the wind flaring it into ashes.

"Know what I'd like to do?" I said. "I think I'd like to be an organizer."

"And organize what?"

"People. Working people."

"Where did you get that idea?"

"Grandpa, I guess. In the old country he was in a union called the Bund, made up of Jewish workers. It was pretty exciting, from what he says. After a long time of being kicked around, the Jews got together, at least the workers did. They wouldn't take it lying down anymore. In one place, a textile town called Lodz, they got to be pretty powerful. Grandpa says it made a new man out of him."

"Is your father like him?"

"No. Pa left the old country and came here when he was young, before all that stuff started, I guess. Grandpa and

Grandma didn't want to come. So when the Bund took hold, they were carried along with it. He says what happened then, that's the difference between him and Pa."

"Oh, Joey, I hope my dad doesn't change. I want him to be the way he always was!"

"Grandpa once told me he wished they'd all stayed in the old country. But then he remembered about Grandma and he said, 'I take that back.'"

"What did he mean?"

"His son—my pa—had gone to America by then. He wanted to pay passage to get him and Grandma over. But Grandpa turned them down. A few years later some terrible pogroms broke out. Not the first time—oh, no! It was as though everybody was out to kill Jews again. Grandpa's sure the government started it. He said the Russian czar was scared of a revolution and had the newspapers whip up violent prejudice against the Jews, blaming us for everything wrong. Jews were beaten up on the streets, robbed, raped, butchered with axes, their homes burned down over their heads. Men, women, children—it made no difference. It was a blood craze. It felt like it would never stop, he said. The Jews tried to defend themselves, but the police and the army were on the side of the mobs. When Grandma was killed, and Grandpa crippled, that was the end for Grandpa. He wrote Pa and Ma and said he'd come now if they could help him."

"I wonder," said Kate, "what we'll remember, if we ever grow old."

13

About a week later a letter came for me. I almost never got any mail, so Ma made a fuss about it. She handed it to me when I came in from school. "It's for you, Big Shot," she said. I took the envelope and saw my name and address typed neatly on the front, and on the back, elegantly engraved, the sender's name: Heming & Heming, Attorneys.

It was a polite letter, but the threat was unmistakable. H&H, it said, were the lawyers for Mr. Dillon. I had taken something he valued, they said. And if I didn't return it, all sorts of bad things were in store for me.

Ma watched me read it, and as soon as I stuffed it into my pocket, she said, "Well? Who is it? What do they want?"

"Lawyers," I said. "They heard what a brilliant scholar I am, and since they need young blood, they want to know if I'll let them put me through Harvard Law School."

"Crazy! Now tell me the truth."

"Where's Pa?"

"Sleeping."

"And Grandpa?"

"Out somewhere. You can talk. They won't know."

"It's Dillon, Ma. He's still after whatever was swiped. And his lawyers think it'd be smart for me to return it."

"Only you haven't got it!"

"Right. But they're sure I have."

"So what can you do?"

"Nothing. What should I do?"

"Answer them!"

"What for? There's something fishy. Why don't they arrest me if they're so sure I'm the thief?"

"Joey, maybe you're making a mistake? I told them already you had nothing to do with it. Now *you* tell them. Let them go hunt a crook someplace else."

"I'm not worried, Ma. You'll see."

But I *was* worried. I figured the missing stuff was something Dillon didn't want made public. Didn't this letter prove it? But those lawyers shook me up a little. I stewed over it for a few days, then talked to Kate. She said I ought to find out once and for all whether it really was Hank I'd seen, and if it was, what he'd taken.

So the next day, when classes were over, I followed Hank out of the schoolyard.

"Going home?" I asked.

"What's it to you?"

"Nothing—only I'm going that way, too."

"Who cares?"

"Nobody. But I'd like to talk to you."

"That's something new!"

"Listen, Hank, I'm not to blame. Who's always making nasty cracks?"

He spat on the sidewalk, just missing my shoe.

"What were you doing in Dillon's house that night?"

"You out of your mind? *What* house?"

"Dillon's house—that's what house."

He began walking faster, pulling ahead of me.

"Wait a minute," I said, grabbing his elbow. "You know damn well what I'm talking about."

"Let go! Who the hell do you think you are?" He yanked his arm free.

I grabbed him by the shoulders and pushed him against a fence. Some people passing by stared at us. I locked my right arm around his left and forced him to walk beside me. He was shaking.

"Shut up and listen," I said. "Or I'll turn you over to the cops."

He was gulping in air, as though he had the heaves. When he'd quieted down a little, I said, "I saw you that night, Hank. You know I was on your tail! You jumped out of Dillon's window; I chased you all the way to the wall; you climbed over it, cut your hand on the glass, and got away through that field. And then I saw you in class with your hand in a bandage."

"That's a pack of lies! I don't know what you're talking about. I cut my hand opening a can of tuna!"

"No, you didn't. You cut it on that broken glass on the wall."

"What wall? I never climbed no wall!"

I took a chance with a near lie. "Listen—I *saw* you. And your father was there, too. Think he doesn't know his own son when he sees him?"

He tried to squirm out of my grip. I held tight to his skinny arm. "You're making things up!" he cried. "If my father saw me, how come he never said so?"

"He's your father, isn't he? Would he want to turn you in?"

"I didn't take nothing! *You* took it!"

Now I had him. "Who said anything was taken?"

His face crumpled up. "It ain't worth nothing anyway," he said. "I'd give it back, only I'm scared they'd put me in jail." The tears began flowing.

"Take it easy, Hank," I said. "I don't want to make more trouble for you. Maybe we can figure a way out of this mess. But I have to know what happened."

"My father," he moaned, "he'll kill me!"

"He doesn't know. I was the only one who saw you. He was outside, in the truck. I never told him I thought you were the thief."

"Geez, Joey, why not? You hate my guts!"

"Sometimes I do, Hank. But Newt's a great guy. I didn't want to hurt him."

"Great guy? I hate him!"

"Are you nuts? How can you say that! Geez, at least you can *talk* to him!"

"That's what you think," he said bitterly. "I wish he was dead, too! Like my ma." And he began crying again.

I took out my handkerchief and gave it to him. We were coming up to a Sterling cafeteria, and I fished in my pocket. Two dimes, enough. I steered him inside, sat him down at a corner table, and got us a tray of coffee and doughnuts. Then the story came out.

He went back to when they were living in Lawrence and Newt had lost his old job in the textile mill. "Then we had to move in with my uncle's family," he said. "But when my uncle lost his job, too, we were always getting mad at each other, fighting all the time. So we left. Found a room with a kitchen in a beat-up old tenement. For a while Pa managed to pay the rent out of odd jobs he picked up. Then those stopped coming, and we fell behind. No money for rent, no money for food.

"Ma started taking us down to the police station once a week, you know, where the soup kitchen is. Me and my kid sister, Lucinda; she was going on five. They gave us potatoes and onions and some canned stuff. I think Ma took us kids so maybe they'd feel more sorry for us and give a little more. It wasn't hardly enough to live off of. Pa wouldn't go. He and Ma yelled at each other all the time. He said he was damned if he'd beg for his food. Ma said would he rather we all starved?

"The landlord kept asking for the rent each month, but Pa couldn't make it. Then one day a sheriff came. It was pay or get out. Pa disappeared. Just like that. We couldn't tell where he was. Ma and me went all over the neighborhood but couldn't find him nowhere. I guess the landlord gave up on kicking us out, because he never did.

"We were all sleeping in that one little room, Ma and Lucinda in the bed, and me on a cot. Ma'd sold the rest of our stuff long ago. I'd wake up sometimes and hear her talk to herself and then cry in the dark. There wasn't nothing I could do, so I pulled the cover over my head."

He stopped, took a bite of his doughnut, chewed once or twice, then fished the pulpy stuff out of his mouth and put it down on the tray.

"One day we went out to the police station to get some food, and on the way back we saw Pa across the street. He was walking with some woman, his arm around her. I let out a yell and started after him. But Ma grabbed me. 'It's not your father,' she kept saying. 'It's not. It's only another man who looks like him.'

"We went to bed that night the way we always did, early, because there wasn't nothing to do and the electric had been turned off anyway.

"I must have been asleep a long time, my head buried under the blanket. Then I woke up, feeling sort of choked and dopey like. There was a funny smell in the room. I wondered what it could be. Then suddenly I knew. It was gas. I crept to the bed and touched Lucinda. She didn't move. So then I shook her harder and harder. She wouldn't move. Where was Ma? By now I could see a little better in the dark. Lucinda looked funny—sort of stiff, and her eyes glassy. The smell in the room was so awful, it was hard for me to breathe. I got to the window, choking and coughing, and it was locked. I felt so woozy, it was hard to do, but I got it open and let the air in. Then I made it into the kitchen.

"There was Ma, sitting on a chair at the table. She looked asleep. All the gas jets of the stove were going, but they weren't lit. I turned them off and broke the kitchen window with a pot. Then I went back to Ma. Her head was drooping to one side. I tried to lift it, but it just flopped back. I noticed in her lap she had a magazine with the pages open. *Airplane Stories*, it was, a thing Pa used to read. I shook her like crazy, slapped her face, yelled in her ear. She just slid off the chair and onto the floor.

"I couldn't call for help—we had no telephone. So I banged on a neighbor's door downstairs, and soon the place was full of cops and ambulance men. It wasn't any use. . . ."

They took him to the police station, Hank said, and in the morning put him in an orphanage. The papers were full of the story, and a few days later Newt showed up and claimed him. Hank didn't want to go with his father, but the police made him. For almost a year Hank never spoke to his father. Newt tried to make it up to him, but Hank wouldn't let him. Then Newt decided they'd better leave the place where it all happened and go somewhere else. That's how they came to Worcester.

"People think we get along," Hank said. "It's only because I couldn't keep saying nothing all the time. But I don't *tell* him anything. He kept after me to help out on the truck. Finally, I did. But I busted every bottle I could. So then he took you."

How'd that make me feel? Rotten.

"That's why I sneaked into Dillon's place," he said. "I knew about when you'd get there on the milk route, and I figured out if I could get in just a couple minutes ahead and swipe something, you'd be blamed for it."

"But what did you take?"

"I don't know."

"You don't know? What kind of a fool do you think I am?"

"I'm telling you, Joey, I *don't* know what it is. I climbed through a window they left unlocked and started to look around. But it was awful dark, and I couldn't hardly see nothing. I didn't have much time. I knew you'd be coming with the milk any second. There were lots of things in the room, so many I thought nobody'd miss anything even if I took it. Then I spotted a box, a little one, sitting on a kind of small stand. It was all by itself. So I figured it must be important even if it was small. I grabbed it and stuck it in my pocket, but I was so jittery, I knocked over the stand. I started back for the window. Before I got to it, I could hear someone running through the hall. I jumped out and began ducking through the bushes, heading for the wall. That's when that guy, whoever he was, reached the window and flashed his light all over the ground."

"But what about the box? What was in it?"

"I told you, I don't know."

"But you opened it!"

"I didn't—I can't!"

This was hard to believe. "You mean you went to all that risk and don't even know what you swiped?"

He was exasperated with himself as well as with me. "I'm no dope, Joey! I tried to open it, but it's locked up. I'm afraid if I bust it open, whatever's inside will break. And then I'd be in even worse trouble."

"Let me look at it?"

He put his hand in his mackinaw pocket and drew out a little box.

"You carry it around with you?" I said.

"Course I do! If I didn't keep it on me all the time, *he'd* find it."

The box was made of some dark kind of wood. Hank put it in my hand. The wood felt silky smooth, as though it had been handled a lot for a long time. I was fascinated by its strangeness, and I began to turn it around.

"For crissakes! Not here!"

I hastily shoved the box into my pocket. "Where, then?" I said.

"Can I trust you?" And before I could answer, he burst into tears again. I was stunned. This kid always acting tough, the wise guy. And he's crying?

"Oh, Joey, Joey. I'm a mess. Why did I do such a stupid thing? To get you blamed for it? Because my father likes you better than me? He hardly says a word to me. And I've felt so alone since my mother and Lucinda . . ."

I felt helpless. What comfort for such a loss? "Hank, let me hang on to the box. I'll find some way to get into it, and then maybe figure out what to do with it. Without getting us in any more trouble."

He drew a deep breath and put out his hand. I put my arm around his shoulder. "So long, Hank. I'll see you soon."

After supper that night I went into our bedroom to wait until I was sure everyone had gone to sleep. Then, careful not to waken Grandpa, I took the little box out of my mackinaw and slithered onto the back porch, the place where Pa kept the tools of his trade. I found what I was looking for, a small steel scraper Pa used to get rid of paint on windows.

I placed the little box on the porch shelf and looked for some spot where I could insert the edge of the scraper. It seemed hopeless, until I felt with a fingernail a tiny indentation on one end of the box. I inserted the scraper and levered it up and down, up and down, gently, so as not to break the box. And then suddenly the thing popped open! There, on a tiny bed of what felt like velvet, was a crucifix—a cross with the smallest figure of Jesus on it. I couldn't believe someone had been able to work on such a tiny scale. It glittered like gold in the moonlight.

Why would Mr. Dillon want this back so urgently? It must be very valuable, maybe an example of a miniaturist's work in medieval times? Still, Dillon hadn't spoken publicly about his loss, and if he was so sure I had stolen it from him, why hadn't he had me arrested?

I closed the box and put a thin strip of tape around it to hold it tight. What could I do about it? I went back into our room, slipped the box into my mackinaw pocket, and went to bed.

During the night I came suddenly wide awake. I was remembering a feature article I'd read in the newspaper quite a while ago. It told about Interpol, an international police force that was on the lookout for priceless things stolen from museums or private collections. The story went on to say how hard it was for the thieves to sell their stolen art. Because art experts knew of these objects, if someone bought one from a thief, he didn't dare show it off or sell it or donate it to a museum. Everyone in the art world would recognize that he had knowingly done something unlawful.

No wonder Mr. Dillon had tried to get back the crucifix without making a public fuss over it—or having me arrested.

I couldn't wait to see Hank.

At recess I called him aside and told him I'd found what was in the box and that I'd figured out the whole story. Hank was astonished, said he'd love to see the crucifix. No, I told him, leave it be.

Then he came up with a great idea, simple but great. "Let's put the box with the crucifix in a little package. Pad it enough inside to hold the little box tight, and then take it to some mailbox far from your home or mine and drop it in. With stamps on it, of course, and Dillon's address. But no return address!"

Great idea! That way neither of us would get into trouble, and the old man would call off the pressure.

So that's what we did. The very next day we walked from our side of town to the west side, almost skipping, we were so pleased with our way out of a nasty situation. We popped our little package into the mailbox, then turned and laughed. "Bet old Dillon will be surprised!" Hank said. When we walked back to our side of town, we came up to a do-it-yourself photo shop. "Hey, let's get mug shots," Hank said. "Spare cops the trouble."

We stood side by side in the booth, and *snap!* The guy developed it for us right away, and there were our smiling faces on the glossy paper. I paid the man fifty cents, and Hank said, "You keep it. Your mug's prettier."

14

By mid-May the papers were reporting that the Bonus Army was sweeping into Washington from everywhere. The vets marched in old suits, bib overalls, or pieces of Army uniforms topped off with khaki overseas caps. They carried knapsacks or duffel bags or bedrolls. They moved in battered old jalopies, in trucks, on freight trains that hundreds jumped aboard at local stops. Along the way friendly folks handed out sandwiches, coffee, and doughnuts, and soon restaurants and bakeries, too, were offering food. As the gathering tide rolled into the Midwest, people were startled to see that many veterans had brought along their wives and kids.

So many were out of work! Chicago, a bankrupt city with 624,000 unemployed. St. Louis, where two thirds of the workforce had lost their jobs. Frightened by the mass desperation, one mayor issued an order banning all demonstrations by the unemployed. A reporter asked him, What are you scared of? A revolution?

When I joined Newt Friday night, he burst out,

"How about that, Joey! Us vets are gonna storm that city! Wish I could be there!" But he couldn't. He was one of the lucky vets who had a job he could count on.

Saturday I got up late. Ma and Pa were still sitting around the table, drinking coffee, Grandpa reading the paper. I sat down and helped myself to a bowl of oatmeal Ma had kept warm for me. Grandpa looked up, slapping the paper.

"Look at this!" he said. It was a picture of veterans with their families on the road in Pennsylvania. "And they're *walking* to Washington."

He handed the paper to Ma. "Nashville, Tennessee," she said, reading the story. "Two thousand veterans on the way. North Carolina, veterans white and Negro coming down from the mountains to walk north to the capital. And get this: One man in Wisconsin is riding on his Big Chief motorcycle. Countless other loners heading to Washington on their own, the paper says."

Pa took the paper from Ma. He turned to the editorial page and found a big cartoon, taking half the sheet, showing zillions of tiny figures swarming like ants on all roads leading to Washington. "It's like in war," he said. "Everyone on the march to where the action is, no one knowing what's gonna happen next. . . ."

"But it's gotta be good, right, David?" said Grandpa. "This time no bullets, no blood. A battle for something you deserve for what you went through. How can anyone turn you down? What did those politicians do? They sat on their butts while you went through hell. They'll *have* to give what they promised!"

"What was the promise, Pa?"

"Years ago, Joey—1924, I think—Congress okayed paying us vets a bonus for our service. But not till 1945. The government said it would be too hard on the treasury to pay us any sooner."

Ma interrupted: "That was okay then, but God knows how many veterans are jobless and hungry right *now*. They need it *now!* And we could use it, too!"

Sunday afternoon—my time with Kate—we walked to the park to sit in the sun. "I wish my dad were here," she said. "We miss him so much. But he doesn't dare take time off his job to visit us. And he no longer has his car to drive back. He's had to sell it so he can keep sending us some money each week. He keeps asking about school, worried that it might shut down if things get even worse. Out where he is, the towns are so short of income from taxes that they're cutting school hours, firing teachers, or cutting their pay. . . ."

That was beginning to happen right here, too, in our own town. Some schools had been shut down altogether, and the kids got jammed into other schools that were already overcrowded. Luckily, our high school, which aimed at preparing kids for college, had not yet been touched. Maybe because so many of the kids came from middle- or upper-class families—and their parents had pull with the politicians.

"Your dad, Kate, was he in the war?"

"No. He has what they call a congenital heart condition, and the medics ruled him out. Why do you ask?"

"Well, I thought he might be in line for that bonus promised to the vets. You know, the papers have been full of stories about what's going on now in Washington."

"Yes," she said. "I know. I haven't forgotten what you've told me about your father. And Mr. Newton, too."

She opened her schoolbag and took out the lunch she'd prepared for us. Our bench was at the pond's edge. I closed my eyes and remembered the way we'd flown across it on our skates in January.

15

Toward the end of the spring term Miss Larkin introduced our class to a Massachusetts writer, Henry David Thoreau. "You've enjoyed Mark Twain and Emily Dickinson this year," she said, "and though Henry is not on the curriculum, I'm hoping some of you will want to read him over the summer vacation."

He had died some seventy years ago, she told us, and in obscurity, hardly noticed by the literary world. Yet since then his major work, *Walden,* had become more and more widely recognized as a masterpiece. She opened the copy on her desk and said, "Let me read you just one passage. You'll see that at heart he was first and always a naturalist—a poet of nature. He could fall in love with a scrub oak or a woodchuck. And this love of nature overflowed into his writing. Just listen to his response to the coming of spring:

"The first sparrow of spring! The year beginning with younger hope than ever! The faint silvery warblings heard over the partially bare and moist fields from the bluebird, the song sparrow, and the red-wing, as if the last flakes of winter tinkled as they fell! . . . The brooks sing carols and glees to the spring. The marsh hawk, sailing low over the meadow, is already seeking the first slimy life that awakes. The sinking sound of melting snow is heard in all dells, and the ice dissolves apace in the ponds. The grass flames up on the hillsides like a spring fire . . . as if the earth sent forth an inward heat to greet the returning sun; not yellow but green is the color of its flame;—the symbol of perpetual youth, the grass-blade, like a long green ribbon, streams from the sod into the summer, checked indeed by the frost, but anon pushing on again, lifting its spear of last year's hay with the fresh life below. . . . So our human life but dies down to its root, and still puts forth its green blade to eternity."

As Miss Larkin closed the book, my eyes sought out Kate's. She smiled lovingly.

"If any of you like what you've heard, you can get a paperback copy of *Walden* very cheaply. But that isn't the reason I think Thoreau's specially important to us now. You've heard about the war veterans down in Washington? Asking for immediate payment of the bonus promised to them? Well, you know they're doing what Thoreau did way back in the 1840s. He'd always been against slavery. So he refused to pay his taxes to a government that supported slavery, that was right then waging a war against Mexico to extend slave territory. Result? He was thrown into jail. That led to his writing the essay 'On Civil Disobedience.'"

A hand went up. "But Miss Larkin, what's that got to do with the Bonus Army?"

"A lot," she said. "The veterans believe our government has a moral obligation to them. To pay the promised bonus, and to pay it now, when they need it desperately. And when the government refuses to honor that obligation, the veterans have a right, a duty, to disobey orders—from the police, or the army, or even the president—to quit demonstrating and get out of Washington."

I could see that wasn't an easy thing to accept. One kid challenged her: "The law's the law, isn't it? Break it and you're punished. That's what everyone says!"

"Well, not always, Sam. People can vote to change a law they believe is unjust. Thoreau holds that you have an obligation to disobey a law that violates your conscience. And if they jail you for it, your protest may awaken others to what's wrong and make them willing to change it." And then she added, "He was for peaceful resistance, nonviolent resistance."

That night at supper I told my folks about how Miss Larkin had linked Thoreau to the vets' campaign. "I can see why she has a special interest in that," Ma said. "I remember that during the war, her brother refused to fight. He was a pacifist and didn't mind telling the world that violence made no sense as a way to settle differences, whether between people or between countries. So they made him serve in a military hospital instead of in battle. That's when it got into the paper."

"And don't forget, Ruth," Grandpa put in, "that other men refused to do even that. They'd have no part of war, no way. And those guys they put in prison."

"That's right," Ma said. "Remember how some people called them traitors? Must have been pretty hard on their families. No wonder your teacher thinks about it," she said, turning to me.

Our senior year was nearing its end, but little fuss was being made over plans for graduation. The seniors from well-off families, yes, they were set for college. Kate? She thought only of how to find work to keep her family going.

As for me, my hope—and it was a pretty thin one— was an idea Miss Larkin had for me. She'd learned that Columbia University's Teachers College was going to launch an experiment in the fall. They planned to open a small college that would prepare students to become teachers. This New College, as it was called, was going to test new kinds of courses and methods proposed by advanced thinkers in the field of education.

"I think you're a natural candidate for it," Miss Larkin said to me. "And I'm going to see if we can't get you a scholarship for this new program."

Of course, I was terrifically excited, but I didn't believe it could really happen. Anyhow, I got the college application forms and filled them out with my school grades and the personal essay they asked for. On a separate sheet I said I'd need a scholarship, and not only that but a job as well, to pay for my meals and dormitory room.

With summer coming on, Pa's work kept thinning out more and more. About all he had left were the homes of a few rich families who didn't need to save pennies. And the Sterling cafeterias. I could count on my work with Newt to bring in fifty cents each night. But we needed help. Ma was in debt to more than one store for stuff we simply had to have.

Then a lucky break came my way. Coming off Newt's truck early one morning, I ran into Gus Reed just leaving for work. He ran the warehouse grocery company, and his family owned our three-decker. He lived on the first floor.

"Hey, Joey," he said. "You got a job? I mean besides that milk route?"

"No, wish I did."

"Well, here's your chance. We need a stockboy down at the warehouse. The kid we had—his family's moving to Boston."

"Gee, that sounds great! What would I do?"

"Simple. Don't have to have brains! Of course I know you have some, because your mom is always bragging about you. What this job calls for is more muscle than mind. You use a hand truck to wheel the crates and cartons and boxes coming into our loading dock to the place where they belong inside. And the other way around—from inside the warehouse to where our delivery trucks pick them up for the grocery stores."

"I could do that! Easy!"

"Well, the job's yours. Start a week from Monday, okay?"

"Sure. What does it pay, Gus?"

"How about fifteen cents an hour? You'd work eight hours a day Monday through Friday. And that'd leave you clear for your milk route Friday and Saturday nights."

Quick arithmetic: fifteen cents times forty hours? Equals six dollars a week. Not bad!

"I like it, Gus." We shook hands on the deal.

A week to go before school let out and my new job would start, I cornered Kate after class to tell her the good news, and I found she had news for me. Her folks used to send her to summer camp every year. That was out now, of course. (When she'd told me that, I'd felt guilty because I was so glad we'd be seeing each other all summer.)

"It's good you'll be working, Joey. And so will I."

"Where, Kate, where?"

"Right here in town. You know the family that lives next to us, the Rogerses? Who own that drugstore in the next block? Well, Mrs. Rogers is expecting a baby, and it's suddenly turned into a risky pregnancy. Doctor says she must quit standing on her feet all day and stay quietly at home or the baby will be at great risk. So she came yesterday to ask if I'd take over her work for the summer months. She handles the cash register and the over-the-counter sales. Mr. Rogers is the pharmacist. I'll get ten dollars a week! My mom's delighted. She wrote Dad right away to tell him the news."

We began walking to the Harrington corner, where our paths toward home separated. Suddenly, we heard loud voices shouting, chanting. There in front of City Hall was a big crowd of men and women. "We're hungry! We need jobs! We want work! Give us food!"

The demonstrators carried hand-lettered signs calling for free coal, free food, free clothing for needy families. One man, standing on top of a little folding ladder, was yelling up toward the windows of the mayor's office: "Put us to work! We don't want charity! We want jobs!"

Three policemen shoved through the crowd and yanked the man down. I heard them say, "Go home, go home. The mayor's heard you. Enough. Enough."

The protesters began to move off. No one was arrested. I knew the cops had seen all this more than once. They were tired; the crowd was tired. Three years of what we were all calling the Great Depression. How long, Lord, how long?

I turned to Kate. We hugged tightly, and I kissed her cheek. "A least we've got work," she said.

16

On the last day of school, Kate and I went up to Miss Larkin's desk to say goodbye and wish her a happy summer. "Stay in touch," she said to me. "The New College people tell me they won't be able to make final decisions on student scholarships till early fall. Getting this project off the ground is proving to be far more difficult than they thought." She added that she'd be staying at her brother's place on Lake Quinsigamond, just outside Worcester. "It's so peaceful there. No students to pester you every minute." And she laughed. "I'm glad you two will have jobs. I guess I should feel lucky I'm not married, or I'd be out of work, too!"

A sad joke, I thought. The city's budget was so squeezed that women teachers who were married were all let go. The theory? Husbands could support them, so give the jobs to other women.

I found I liked my new job. It kept me so busy that I had little time to think about the scholarship. There were only a few other men in the warehouse, all of them lots older than me. They often made wisecracks about what kids know—or had better not know.

They showed me how to balance my weight to shift the loads around. But if once in a while one of them saw that I had too much to handle, he would run up to help me. My arms and legs, my back, too, felt the strain at first, and I ached in bed at night. But there was nothing bad enough to make me think I'd be better off running errands on a bike or something.

I had no idea of the cost of the bulk products the company sold. What I did know was the prices at our corner grocery: eggs were nineteen cents a dozen; lettuce, a nickel a head; whole wheat bread, a nickel a loaf; bananas, eight cents a dozen; mackerel, two pounds for twenty-five cents; beef, eleven cents a pound; and tomato soup, three cans for nineteen cents.

As I walked home with Gus after work one day, he told me he wished the company could cut their wholesale prices so that more people could afford the food they needed. "But the profit margin's already so thin, we're lucky to stay in business."

When I told Kate this, she said her drugstore, too, was skating on thin ice. Mr. Rogers said he knew that many of his customers must be taking lower doses of the medicines their doctors prescribed. "You know, cutting the pill in half. Or taking it every third day instead of daily." Why? Because they couldn't afford to renew their prescriptions—even when they knew this would hurt their chances of recovery from whatever sickness they had.

Summer seemed to be passing so quickly. It was a real hot one. I often worked in shorts and a T-shirt. My night shifts with Newt weren't much cooler. Kate and I were able to take the trolley out to Lake Park on Sunday afternoons for a swim. That part of the lake was full of swimmers and boaters. You had to steer your way clear of them.

On one of those Sundays we began to talk about what was next for us. Kate had been sure of college. Her folks had gone—to the best ones, at that—and of course expected that she would, too. She knew better now. Her mom kept insisting they'd find a way to get her into Smith or Radcliffe, even if it took another year. "But how?" Kate said. "With what money?" Even if she won a scholarship for tuition, she'd still need to pay for room and board, plus books and everything else.

As for my own chances, they looked like zero. I didn't really believe a scholarship would come through. In the old country no one in my family had gone to school, much less college. My folks had learned English the hard way, by trial and error, and they were still learning. Yet my ma acted as though she had a sacred obligation to see that her son went to college.

Kate rolled over to me on our beach towel, and I held

her close. "Kate, Kate, if only it would come true! This can't go on forever! It's nearly three years since the roof fell in. Times can't stay this way forever! We'll find a way out—we've just got to!"

At home we were all following the news closely. Most of the vets who'd flocked into Washington back in May were still there. And they were being joined by thousands more. They were making do in all sorts of odd places—in public parks, in abandoned houses, in empty lots. Many had built what looked like chicken coops out of packing crates, junked shutters, old newspapers, tarpaper, strips of cardboard scraped out of the city dumps. "Hoovervilles," people called these communities—because President Hoover had done almost nothing to help people who were starving and couldn't afford to live in a home. Hoovervilles had sprung up all over the country.

One reporter pointed out that in these Washington Hoovervilles Negroes and whites were living, cooking, and eating together. For years, the reporter said, the U.S. Army had argued that General Jim Crow was its proper commander. Maybe that old notion was wrong? I wondered. Lots of people still thought Jews weren't good enough to live in the same neighborhood with Christians. When would that stop? When would Jim Crow be ended?

For a while things seemed to be looking up: Congress got ready to vote on the bill to pay out the veterans' bonus, right away, and in cash. It would amount to an average of about three hundred dollars per vet. One Congressman demanded to know how anyone could turn his back on veterans who asked only for a dollar a day, for bread for themselves and their families. "They ask it from the wealthiest country in the world," he said, "for which they fought. A million or more are in dire need. They ask for bread, and Congress should not offer them a stone."

Then for a while there was hope. The House of Representatives passed the bill, by a vote of 209 to 176. "We won on that front," Newt said. "Now for the battle in the Senate."

Two days later thousands of veterans advanced on Capitol Hill to remind the Senate what this fight was all about. Calling up a line from the old Army song "The Yanks Are Coming," someone began singing loudly, "The Yanks are starving," and everyone joined in. It must have battered the ears of those senators.

Debate on the bill continued all afternoon and into the night. At home we kept our ears glued to the radio. Finally, around nine thirty P.M. came the news flash— the bill had been overwhelmingly defeated in the Senate. We were stunned. The newscaster said, "It looks as if there might be an attack on the Capitol!" Then someone shouted, "Sing 'America.'" And the veterans all joined in. We could hear their voices faintly over the air. As the last notes faded, the voice on the radio said the vets were drifting back to their scattered shacks.

The next day our newspaper ran an editorial saying how happy it was that the vets hadn't rioted over that negative vote. They thought it "amazing." And then it dished out advice. "Admit defeat, and go back home."

Was that editor wrong! Sure, some veterans with their families left the next day. But most settled in for a long siege of Congress. And within days thousands more trooped into Washington to add their strength.

But what could be done? I wondered. Congress wouldn't come back until the fall of 1932—after the elections. By now Franklin Delano Roosevelt had been chosen as the Democratic candidate for president. He'd been the governor of New York for one term. He was crippled with polio but was managing just the same. Wouldn't any president be better than Hoover? I asked Pa.

"Not so sure," Pa said. "So far he's said nothing to back the bonus bill."

Day after day in the unrelenting July heat everyone seemed to think of nothing but the Bonus Army camped near the Capitol. Most of them had gathered at Anacostia Flats. What was happening was always page 1

117

news. The government offered a few dollars to every vet who would leave the city. Only a fraction took the money and left.

One day we read that Major General Smedley Butler, a retired Marine Corps veteran who angered the top brass for always sticking up for the enlisted men, had talked to a crowd of five thousand veterans. "Hang together," he said, "and stick it out till the gate bars of hell freeze over; if you don't, you are no damn good. . . . Remember, by God, you didn't win the war for a select class of a few financiers!" He urged them to go to the polls in November and change things. "And don't do anything lawless," he said, "or you'll lose the sympathy of the people."

Soon there was big trouble when groups of vets began picketing federal buildings, shouting out their slogans, their need for a bonus now, right now. The police moved in on them with nightsticks, and the vets tried to fend them off with their fists. It ended when squads of motorcycle cops roared in and scattered the veterans.

That did it for Army Chief of Staff General Douglas MacArthur. All along he'd charged that these were only gangs of Reds out to make trouble, and the government was much too tolerant of them. That accusation angered all of us, especially Pa. "What right does that guy have, with all his ribbons and medals, to talk like this? And him with his big-shot pay? Is he having trouble paying the rent? Putting food on the table?"

I hadn't seen him so mad in Lord knows when. And when I met Newt on my shift Friday night, I found he was boiling over, too. "I've got to join the guys down there," he said. "It's a shame for any of us to stay home and let other vets fight for us. I'm gonna drive down Monday, and Hank's coming along, too. He says if lots of the vets have their kids with them, then he should go, too. People will see it's whole families in trouble, not just the vets.

"How about your pop? Is he ready to go? I can take him easy. Ask him!"

I did. The next morning. And to my delight, Pa said, "Yes! I should do my part, too. I'll call Newton. I'll go, I'll go."

"And me, too!" I almost yelled. "Hank's going, and why not me?"

Ma didn't look very happy with that. But she said nothing. Maybe she thought the more the merrier. Or the safer. Then, "What about the Sterling cafeterias, David? They're almost your only job left. Who'll do their windows with you gone?"

"Don't worry, Ruth. I'll arrange with my old sidekick Bill Reddick to carry on those few days while we're gone. The Sterling people know him. It'll be okay."

That made me think about Newt's milk route, and

my job, too. I guessed he'd be able to have one of the other company drivers take over a route that had shrunk these last months. I'd been expecting Newt would lay me off any time now.

Gus was just leaving our yard when I caught up with him. I blurted out the news about Pa and me joining the Bonus Army in Washington. "So you want time off?" he asked. "Okay. I can get one of the warehouse men to bring in his son while you're gone."

He paused, then added, "Maybe you forgot, or maybe didn't know. That's how I lost my dad, in that same damn war. Very first day in combat. Let me do something, too. Pull up at the warehouse on your way out, and we'll load on some food for the vets down there."

I phoned Kate that night to tell her we were leaving the next day. She was startled—and worried, like everyone else. She was following the Bonus Army stories in the paper and on the radio.

"But why would *you* go, Joey? You're no vet! Your pa, that's one thing. But you, too? The paper says the government people are just looking for an excuse to force the vets out of Washington. And that smells to me like violent stuff. My mother says either the vets get so frustrated, so mad, they start a riot, or the army and the police will provoke fighting to give them the excuse they're looking for to force the vets out of Washington."

I knew she was right. Grandpa, too—he was guessing that might happen. He'd seen it long ago, in the old country.

"It could happen, Kate, it could. But if men like Pa and Newt don't fight for what they deserve, what they *need*, who will?"

"You're right. But why do you and Hank need to go?"

"Because it's about us, all of us. What we need. What Pa's owed. And maybe, come another war someday—God forbid!—the big shots will remember this, and treat us decently."

She sighed. "All right, Joey. Be careful! And promise me you'll phone so I know you're all right. Call collect—it'll be easier."

17

---•◆•---

I slept badly that night, and at dawn I packed the old knapsack I'd used in the brief time I'd been a Boy Scout. I managed to squeeze in an extra set of underwear, two pairs of socks, a denim shirt, my rain jacket, a cap, and of course a toilet kit. I figured I could get by on the dungarees Ma complained I lived in.

The drive to Washington was no big deal. Pa sat next to Newt up front in the truck, and Hank and I squatted down on the floor in back, groaning over every bump in the road. When we got there by late afternoon, we headed for Anacostia Flats, where we knew thousands of vets were camping in their tents or makeshift shacks.

At the camp kitchen we unloaded the food Gus had given us. A cook grinned thanks. "New people? Expect two meals a day, if we're lucky. You wanna wash up? There's the river, our bathtub. Not exactly like home. Polluted, 'cause a sewer upstream empties into it."

We saw people cooking in army field kitchens the district police chief, a guy named Pelham Glassford, had wangled for the vets. Camp Marks, they called this place. Named after another friendly police officer, we were told.

Pinned to a bulletin board we saw a news clipping. It said a Father James R. Cox had just been here. A priest from Pittsburgh, he'd led a march of jobless men back at home and had just driven in to speak to the vets. "Stick it out!" he'd cried. "You'll never get what you're entitled to unless you stick. Men are coming from every corner of the country, and if you stick it out, before this is over there'll be from half a million to a million of you. If they won't give you this little bonus offered you because your wartime pay was less than common labor—turn them out of office! Go home and organize against them. Send men here who still look after the people, not the five hundred millionaires who control the national wealth."

In the months since the camp had sprung up, a community life had taken hold. Not only where we were parked but in two dozen other places as well—abandoned buildings, parks, empty lots. The settlements were built of cardboard, egg crates, wrecked cars, and bed springs. Camp Marks, the biggest, was the heart of the Bonus Army.

As we settled into a lean-to we put up next to Newt's truck—made of blankets and raincoats we'd brought along—we could feel the anxiety in the air. Government officials had just ordered that the vets and their families must be cleared out of all federal property, beginning with a camp in the center of town. It didn't look good for raggedy people to be camping within sight of the White House, the newspapers said. The aim was to push us onto privately owned land, where many vets had already built shantytowns.

The first target of the government was a stretch of Pennsylvania Avenue, close by Capitol Hill and only half a mile from the White House. Demolition gangs had been tearing down old buildings to clear the way for construction of new government buildings. But now these empty shells were filling with Bonus marchers, and on the surrounding empty lots were the shacks and lean-tos of other veterans.

That first night in camp I didn't sleep much. We lay on blankets we'd brought from home. There were sounds of people talking, babies crying, engines sputtering. Up at daylight, we threw together a cold breakfast and got hot coffee from the camp kitchen. I wondered what would happen next. Then, over the amplifiers, we heard the news: The police had begun to clear out the Pennsylvania Avenue encampment, urging the vets to leave peacefully. We joined hundreds of others rushing to the city center to support our guys under siege.

When we reached the wrecking site, we found the police had pushed the watching crowds back and roped off the battleground. They still hadn't hauled all the vets out of some of the buildings. From the street we looked up to see two officers struggling with men on a second floor. The outer wall had been demolished. Suddenly, bricks and stones flew through the air, hitting the cops. One of them, staggering in a daze, somehow got his gun out and fired two shots. I trembled at the sound of the gun going off. The bullets struck two veterans. We could see cops making their way down the broken stairs, bearing two bodies, blood trickling over them. The crowd groaned and sobbed.

"One of our guys is dead!" a vet close by shouted.

Both victims were rushed away in an ambulance. We later learned from the evening newspapers brought into the camp that the first to die was a thirty-seven-year-old veteran from Chicago, and the other, soon dead, too, was a thirty-eight-year-old veteran from Oakland, California.

"What'll happen now?" I asked.

"Anybody's guess," Newt said. "I bet General MacArthur will clamp down with martial law so he can do whatever he wants to get rid of us."

Sure enough, as we milled around on the avenue, we heard the *clop-clop* of horses, and about two hundred cavalrymen pounded up, followed by army trucks out of which many infantrymen jumped. Some of the crowd cheered, while we joined others in booing. Meanwhile, lots of spectators had slipped into the street, resisting the police, who kept shoving them back onto the sidewalk and yelling, "Go home! Go home!"

We couldn't believe it when flatbed trucks roared up, loaded with five army tanks. Pa and Newt kept sizing up the military display. "Look! They're carrying tear-gas grenades!"

Around four o'clock a one-star general standing beside General MacArthur called the infantry, cavalry, and tank officers to attention. He announced that the "so-called" Bonus Marchers were occupying government properties and resisting efforts to evacuate them. "You are commanded to use such force as is necessary to accomplish your mission. Tear gas will be used," he said. He then cautioned the troops to show women and children in the area "every consideration and kindness."

By now the area was flooded with people, ten thousand at least. Here and there were vets carrying signs:

HERE WE STAY TILL THE BONUS THEY PAY!

MILLIONS FOR WAR:
NOT ONE CENT FOR THE HUNGRY VET!

WHO WON THE WAR!
WE HAVEN'T WON ANYTHING!

The infantry drew up and fixed their bayonets while the cavalry herded the bystanders to the north and us vets to the south. Newt yelled, "The last time I saw bayonets, I was fighting in France!"

A cavalry officer shouted, "You got three minutes to clear out! Three minutes! I warn you!"

As the soldiers put on their gas masks, someone in the crowd flung a stone at them. All hell broke loose. We four huddled together, Pa clutching my hand as though I were still a child. What to do? Where to hide? Infantrymen rushed past us into the wrecked buildings, where some vets remained, and tossed tear-gas grenades down the stairwells to force them out. A sudden rising wind carried clouds of the tear gas out on the street, making us cough and choke.

Why was the army carrying on like this was war? What had Pa done, what had Newt done, what had all the vets done to deserve this?

Many vets—tired, weak, sick—couldn't stand the attack and began to run. Pa and Newt grabbed me and Hank, and we ran, too. "No time for heroes!" Pa spit out.

As we turned off the avenue, I looked back and saw the tanks rolling down from the carrier trucks. Infantrymen massed behind us, jabbing bayonets to make us move faster. Then, just as we turned a corner, there was a series of explosions. "What's that? What's that?" I cried to Pa.

"Tear-gas bombs!" he said. "Look! The whole block's on fire! They're burning down all the buildings to force the last guys out!"

And the shanties, too, that vets had patched together on the vacant lots. Vets fled with their families and their few belongings, but some stood their ground, defying the cavalry now charging up with drawn sabers. As bricks flew and sabers slashed, we kept retreating. Finally, all of us exhausted, Pa said, "It's about over. Let's get back to our camp."

It took a long time to tramp back there. When we reached our place, we flopped down in our lean-to. We were too tired to even think about eating. All around us the air was buzzing with talk of what people had seen or done.

I felt wiped out. We all did. But none of us could sleep. Suddenly, we heard a bugle call. We thought it a sour joke. But it was a guy everyone considered to be the camp commander. He was summoning the vets. We ran to where we saw the crowd gathering. A man with a megaphone was yelling: "I never advocated violence! But here it comes—heading right for us! We've got to protect ourselves! Don't blame the police for what's happening! No, we blame the army, we blame the president! If they come to this camp tonight, we'll meet them at the gate. And God pity the first man to put his foot across the line."

He said there were about seven thousand people in our camp now, six hundred of them women and children. He called for volunteers to patrol the edge of the camp, to alert everyone if MacArthur's soldiers marched on us. Pa and Newt stepped up at once and were sent to their posts. Hank and I worked our way through the crowd, back to our lean-to. Darkness had fallen hours earlier. We lay on our blankets, hoping to nap. Hank fell asleep, but I couldn't doze off. I got up and saw vets nearby packing up their stuff. Getting ready to head home, just in case.

Then, in the distance, fires blazed up. Soldiers were moving rapidly down the rows of tents and shanties, using wadded newspapers as torches to set them afire. The camp exploded with terrified screaming, shouting, curses, groans, sobs. Then the soldiers began to sling tear-gas grenades into the panicky mob scrambling for safety.

I grabbed at the soldier nearest to me. "What the hell are you doing? Are you guys crazy? Stop! Stop!"

He looked like a kid, no older than me. His eyes bugged out. "Lemme go! Get out! It's orders! We got a job to do!" And he shoved me off with one arm as he headed down the row to the next tent, his torch flaring.

Frightened, I thought, Where's Hank? Still asleep? I ran back toward our row of shelters. Some of them were already ablaze. I saw Hank wrestling with a soldier, trying to make him drop the torch. As I came near, another soldier raced toward me with his bayonet thrusting, and I turned and ran. Shrinking behind a fiery tent, I looked back toward our lean-to and saw Hank still struggling with the soldier. Suddenly, the soldier freed himself from Hanks's grasp and jabbed furiously at his legs.

Hank screamed and fell to the ground. I ran as fast as I could. Just as I reached them, the soldier turned away and disappeared into the chaos. Hank was out cold. I saw blood gushing from his thigh. "Hank! Hank! Can you hear me? I'll get help! Hold on!" But he couldn't hear anything. . . . Nothing . . .

I tore off my shirt and tried to stop the bleeding. But it was too late. An artery had been slashed, and the blood poured out in a flood. A few minutes later Pa and Newt appeared, breathless from running toward the flaming tents. They could tell in a moment. Hank . . . was gone. Dead.

"Who did this? *Who did this?*" Newt yelled. And he started to move toward the soldiers, who were now beyond the charred and smoldering ruins of the camp.

Pa grabbed and held him. "No use, Newt. They all did this. All of them."

"No," I said. "I did it."

"What? What did you say?" Pa was yelling at me. "Joey! You crazy?"

"No, I could have helped him. But I ran away. . . ."

And I burst into tears, sobbing convulsively, pushing Pa away as he tried to hold me.

Just then an ambulance raced up, and out jumped some medics. They saw Hank crumpled on the ground and, shoving Newt aside, picked him up and tossed him like a sack into the back of the ambulance. I got a fleeting glimpse of the interior—two other bodies piled on the floor.

Neither the driver nor the medics asked who Hank was or what had happened. My bloody shirt was wrapped around his upper leg, but if they noticed it, they said nothing. They swiftly jumped aboard and raced away.

Newt was crazy with grief and anger. Pa kept trying to calm him down, assuring him that tomorrow they'd go to the authorities and claim Hank. Putting an arm around Newt, Pa gently moved him into our lean-to and at last got him to lie down. We twisted and turned on the floor of the lean-to, unable to sleep. Why did Hank die, why didn't I save him, how could I be such a coward? . . .

Hours passed, and when first light came, with Pa and Newt asleep at last, I slipped out of the lean-to. With a pencil stub I scrawled a note along the torn edge of a newspaper, saying I couldn't go home, not now. I had to be alone. I placed the note on the seat of Newt's truck, grabbed my knapsack, and ran off.

To where?

For what?

18

I headed for the bridge into Virginia but saw the entrance was barred by soldiers and state troopers. It was early dawn now, and rain had begun to fall. I saw women with wet handkerchiefs held up to their smarting eyes, and babies crying from the tear gas in their lungs. Behind us the rain was damping down the last flames from the smoldering shelters.

Taking pity on us, the soldiers at last let us cross over the bridge. "Go home! Go home!" they kept yelling.

Cars began to come by, people on their way to work. Some stopped to give a lift to vets thumbing rides, but most others, frightened perhaps, ignored the outstretched hands and kept on going.

I trudged along the highway heading south, barely able to lift one leg and then the other. I was worn to the bone by the sleepless night and soul-sick over Hank's death.

Unable to move another step, I flopped down beside the road. With only a few cars on the road this early, my chance of hitching a ride seemed slim, until a driver braked to a stop, leaned over to my side of the road, said, "Hey, kid! Need a lift?" and beckoned to me to hop in. I dragged myself over, opened the door, and sat down beside him. He told me he was a reporter, assigned to cover the Bonus March.

"A kid like you?" he said. "You're one of the marchers?"

Yes, I told him, and as he continued questioning, I managed to tell him something about Pa and Newt, why they'd joined the Bonus Army, and what we'd seen. But I said nothing about Hank.

"So where you headed now?" he asked.

I couldn't go home, I told him. "No jobs there. I mean to look for work somewhere else. Don't want to give my folks another mouth to feed."

"Look, kid. Jobs aren't plentiful anywhere these days. What'll you do? Just bum around? Too damn many people doing that! And a kid like you? You'll likely end up in jail. Or dead!"

"Maybe, maybe," I said. And then I shut up. He wasn't making me feel any better.

He drove us cross-country through West Virginia, heading for Ohio and his newspaper office in Cincinnati. On the way he stopped at a roadside joint for a meal, generously paying for mine, too. He didn't talk much. Except once when he burst out how he couldn't believe the government would drive vets out of the city with tanks and tear gas and soldiers. "Only good thing is I bet this'll push

Hoover out of the White House and pull Roosevelt in."

When we entered Cincinnati, it was late afternoon. Stopping at a railroad yard on the edge of town, he slipped me a five-dollar bill and said, "So long, kid. Wish you luck!"

Water towers reared up over a rickety fence surrounding the yard. I could see freight cars standing at sidings, waiting to be loaded. I squirmed through a hole in the fence and began to explore the yard. Hearing laughter rising beyond a row of boxcars, I walked around them and found a bunch of kids there.

"Hey! New guy!" one of them said when he caught sight of me. As I came closer, I counted about a dozen kids. Mostly boys and three girls.

"Where you from?" a boy asked.

"Massachusetts."

"How'd you get here?"

"Hitching rides."

"Not riding the rods?"

"No, never done that."

"Well! We'll show you how!"

They asked if I'd eaten yet, and I told them yes, on my last hitch the driver fed me. "And slipped me a fiver, too," I added.

"Wow! What luck!" said one of the girls. "I ain't seen that much dough in years!"

No one asked my name. By now dark was coming on.

They dipped spoons into some sort of stew heating over a makeshift fire. After they finished eating, they began to shift into what comfortable positions they could find—some lying on their tattered jackets flat on the ground, some sitting with their backs against the fence. I took up a space beside one of the boys, keeping one hand in the pocket where I'd stowed the fiver.

The three girls, I noticed, had crept into a small lean-to decked over with tin and held up by three cedar posts. They lay down side by side on a long sack of burlap filled with straw.

The boy next to me asked, "You goin' anyplace special?"

"No. Just anyplace but home. Sick of hanging around there. Maybe better luck someplace else."

"What's your name?"

"Joey. And yours?"

"I'm Al. From Texas."

His face was sunburned tomato red. Must have been riding a lot on the roofs of freights.

I wasn't very comfortable.

"Here," said Al. "Take this newspaper. Roll it up. Makes a pretty good pillow." He was using his crumpled jacket for a headrest.

Didn't take long for him to fall asleep. I couldn't sleep for quite a while, and I lay there wondering about this gang I'd fallen into. I was bothered by mosquitoes and fleas, too. Must have been hours later that I woke, hearing Al muttering in his sleep, as though arguing with somebody.

Then I slept again, until Al shook me awake in daylight. "C'mon," he said. "There's a mission nearby. We can try for breakfast there."

I joined the group and we trudged about a mile to an old church on the edge of town. When we got there, I had to sign my name or they wouldn't feed me. That done, I lined up for breakfast. A bowl of soup, that's all. It was only lukewarm and watery. Not even crackers or a slice of bread to go with it. We sat on hard benches, slopped up the soup, then got out quickly to make way for the line behind us. No second bowl, Al said, even if you're starving.

When we left the mission, I wondered how long I could get by this way. And what about the folks back home? They must be worried sick. I'd better let them know I was all right.

Outside the church our gang gathered to decide what to do next. Some wanted to stay put longer. (They'd been in town about ten days.) But others argued no, let's move on.

We straggled back to the hangout—the "jungle," they called it. I soon found out why this bunch of boys and girls stuck together. "Better," Al said, "than going it alone. Hitchhiking on the road by yourself," he warned me, "makes trouble for you. People won't pick up a dirty beggar. But the police will."

When we settled in again at the clearing near the rail yard, a cleanup began. In a small stream nearby, the guys and girls washed their clothing. Shirts, socks, underwear, pants were hung on bushes to dry in the sun. Mary, a redheaded girl, pretty but awfully skinny, sewed a patch on the seat of a boy's pants while he stood very still. Two guys were trying to figure out how to repair a hole in a shoe.

Around ten o'clock, one of the boys came running up. "Hey! They're getting ready to move the train!"

As a string of boxcars slowly rolled toward us, Al grabbed my hand and yelled, "Stick close! Do what I do!"

Everyone ran out of the grass, ready to swing aboard one of the empties. I saw how Al grabbed a metal bracket on the sliding door and, still running alongside, hauled himself up. I tried it, praying I wouldn't fall, and sure enough managed to swing aboard. In the dim light of the boxcar I saw not only our own bunch but several others, young and old, some with packs, some with tattered suitcases, others with bundles.

I inched my way toward a corner of the boxcar and then, sitting against the smelly wall, tried to fall asleep. But it was nearly impossible. People were chattering, coughing, laughing, crying.

After a while Al made his way toward me. And it was then that I learned something about where he was from and why he was here.

"Texas," he said. "It wasn't bad before the big trouble hit. Somehow we made it, though Dad was never in good shape for work. He'd been in the war and got some sort of sickness. Maybe a whiff of poison gas? But he never got a pension. He'd be sick for about a month each year, lose his job, and have to find another when he was up to it. Even then we didn't do bad till the Depression hit. I had a newspaper delivery route; my brother shined shoes in a barber shop. My sister? She took care of a neighbor's kids. And Mom—she was great with a needle—she did sewing jobs for our neighbors. We even had a Ford, and a radio and a phonograph!

"I'd started high school when the trouble hit. At first we didn't think much about it. Then, all of a sudden, everybody was hard up. Not just us. Seemed nobody could get work. Dad got sicker and sicker. Neighbors couldn't pay for Ma's sewing or my sister's babysitting. My newspaper route faded away when people quit taking the paper."

He was twisting his hands together as he spoke. They were slender and delicate, almost like a girl's, I noticed.

"We tried," he said, "all of us. Dad would do anything, no matter what, or for how little. Mom, always a good cook, tried peddling homemade cake door to door.

No takers. My sister made great wax flowers, but who wanted them now? There was no heat in the house, except just a little while before we went to bed. Dad even gave up smoking. We were down to eating mush— and then I took off."

"You mean you ran away?"

"No. Just quit high school and told my folks I'd move around trying to find work so I could help out, send money home. They didn't like that. My father was mad as hell. I think maybe it made him feel he wasn't up to the job of being a father. Anyway, like it or not, I took off. That was about six months ago. And I've had damn little to send home. Nothing, really."

"Where'd you go?"

"Oh, Fort Worth, Dallas, Houston . . . Same everywhere. Hopped trains on the Hobo Express so often, can't count 'em. But I'm lucky to be here. Alive."

"What do you mean?"

"Well, just a few weeks ago I was riding the rails on my own. And when I couldn't find an empty boxcar, I rode the bumpers. You know, between two cars? I hung on to a brake rod in case my feet slipped. But when I realized I'd fallen asleep, I was terrified. If my hands loosened, I'd fall under the train. So I kept punching my head with one hand to stay awake while I was hanging on with the other. Until the train stopped and I jumped off."

"Thank God you made it alive."

"Yeah, that time. But what about next?"

Just then the freight rattled to a halt. We'd been on the move a few hours, I guessed. No one knew how long we'd stay here. "Let's scram!" one of the guys yelled, and one after another we jumped out the doors, landing on cinders alongside the track.

"Anyone know where we are?" asked Marge.

"Yeah," said Bernie. "Small town. Centerville, I think. We're still in Ohio, for sure. I know of a spot where we can hole up for a while. And there's a convent here, too, if I remember right. Could be a good place to cadge eats, maybe even clothes."

We walked away from the track and in a while reached a farm. I could see an orchard—a lot of fruit on the ground. But it looked untended.

"Farmer must have left off trying," said Al. "Bet he's headed west. I heard there might be work out in California."

There was still some fruit on the trees in the orchard, and we rushed in to pick as much as we could. Result? An orgy of overeating. I thought my gut would explode if I took one more bite.

We took it easy in the barn. It was in pretty good shape. The farmer had not been gone long enough for the roof or walls to cave in. Plenty of hay in the loft, great for bedding. Smelled sweet, too.

"Hey, guys!" It was Bernie calling out. "It's still long

before dark. Anyone want to join me to see what we can bum from the convent?"

A convent? I had never been in one, even near one. "Count me in," I said.

"And me, too." It was Marge. I'd noticed her right off. She was about sixteen, I thought. Plump and pretty. No one else seemed interested in going. So the three of us took off.

About an hour later we were standing at the back door of the convent, a two-story red-brick building.

"Look, guys," said Bernie. "I think Marge should ring the bell, while me and Joey duck around the corner so whoever comes to the door won't see us. Better chance to get something if Marge is alone."

"But I never did this before! I won't know what to say!"

"Oh, you'll know. You need something? Just ask for it."

And that's what happened. We hid, and when Marge pushed the bell, in a minute or two a nun answered. We couldn't hear their talk, but Marge told us she just said, "I'm so hungry—can you help?" And the nun nodded, returned in a few minutes, and handed Marge a brown paper bag.

As soon as Marge reached us around the corner, we opened the bag and found a big loaf of delicious-looking bread, some potatoes, two big tomatoes, a bunch of carrots, and a cake. Then Marge opened her hand. In her palm were two quarters. "How about that!" And she grinned.

"Hey! Not bad!" I said. "You must have acted like a little saint, Marge."

"Yeah," and she blushed. "I hope I don't have to do this too often."

About halfway back to the gang's hangout, walking through a patch of woods, Bernie handed me the bag and said, "You go on. I wanna play with Marge." And moving quickly behind her, he reached around and stroked her breasts.

"Cut that out!" she yelled. "What do you think you're doing! Let me go!"

Laughing, he only grabbed her tighter. I kicked him violently behind his knees and wrenched his arms off her. He turned and took a wild swing at me. I ducked while Marge screamed, "Stop! Stop! Just let me be!" And she ran off toward our camp.

I picked up the brown bag and followed her. Bernie slouched along behind me.

19

Near sunset the next day a new guy wandered in. Good-looking, bronzed skin from too much sun, I figured. But what struck me was the overseas cap he was wearing on top of that mop of curly black hair. Same type of cap that Newt never took off.

"Hey! What's with that vet's cap? Or did they draft babies in that war?"

He grinned. "Naw, it was my father's."

"I wondered. My pop was in that mess, too."

He held out his hand and we shook. Now I was no longer the new kid. Made me feel like an old-timer. The others paid him no heed. "You on the loose? Wanna join up?"

"Yeah, if it's okay."

"Sure. Hungry?"

"No. Packed some sandwiches before I left. Still have a couple left."

"Oh, so you're just starting out?"

"Guess so."

How come was none of my business, he seemed to be telling me. He moved off a way, sat down by himself.

Later that night, with most everyone snoozing, I noticed the new guy had taken out a flashlight and was using it to read a small book. Now, that was the only time I'd seen anyone in our gang with a book. I couldn't help but be nosy. I rolled over toward him and, so I wouldn't wake the others, quietly asked, "What you reading?" He looked up and held the book open so I could see the title page.

The Weary Blues by Langston Hughes.

"My mom bought it for me when I turned thirteen. 'Now that you're a teenager,' she said, 'try this.'"

I knew that book! Aggie Larkin had brought it into class one day. "A poet," she said. "His first book. And judging by his wonderful voice, we'll be hearing lots more of him."

When I told the kid I'd learned about Hughes in school, he was surprised.

"You sure?" he said. "Not pulling my leg? He's a Negro. Bet there were no colored people in your school."

"You're right. Not a one. And none in our neighborhood, either. But I guess my teacher didn't care what color a poet was, so long as he was good. You got a favorite poem?"

"Yeah, many. I'll try this short one on you." And he turned the pages till he found the lines he wanted. He didn't read them aloud, just showed me the poem.

My People

The night is beautiful,
So the faces of my people.

The stars are beautiful,
So the eyes of my people.

Beautiful, also, is the sun.
Beautiful, also, are the souls of my people.

Suddenly the title struck me: "My People" . . . Was this new guy a Negro? Didn't think so when I first saw him, but . . . Somehow he knew what I was thinking.

"Yes," he said, "my people."

And then he added, "I don't know why I'm telling you. Most people don't know. Can I trust you? Don't tell the gang. Or they might kick me out."

"Of course," I said. "I never would."

"My name is Tony Lawson." He held out his hand.

We shook, and I gave him my name.

In the morning, before we broke up to scrounge for whatever, I told the gang that Tony was joining up. You know me. I couldn't wait too long before trying to find out why Tony was on the road. Gradually, in between scavenger hunts, he told me about his father.

"Negro," he said, "and no mistaking it." He was a railroad worker, on the Pennsy. Volunteered before the draft began and ended up in an infantry regiment.

"My mom," Tony said, "looks more like me, was a nurse in a hospital in Maryland. And I was hardly more than a baby when my father took off. Mom told me later she'd tried to keep him home. 'You volunteering to serve in a segregated army? And this is supposed to be a war to make the world safe for democracy? Whose democracy? For whites only?' But he'd argued our people at least have a chance for freedom in a country that promises life, liberty, and maybe happiness, too. That German kaiser. If he won, would we be better off?

"Well, promises, promises," Tony said. "Here it is fourteen years since the war ended. I heard about the Bonus Army. My father's gone. He earned a medal for bravery, but he was wounded badly. Came home nearly a wreck. And died three years later. I barely got to know him. My mom's so worn down by having to work double duty in the hospital—they're always stretching hours because money's so scarce—I don't know, I've tried for work just about everywhere, but nothing doing. So at least now Mom doesn't have to feed me. . . . And maybe somewhere luck will catch up with me."

I wondered to myself how Tony happened to look like he did. Then I remembered reading about slavery times and the way white plantation owners had their way with slave women. I couldn't sleep thinking of what I'd do if that happened to a woman in my family. . . .

20

We stayed in our jungle another few days, scrounging scraps of food at back doors, stealing vegetables from gardens, sometimes missing meals altogether. Then one morning we trudged toward the same railroad yard we'd left—seemed so long ago—and got ready to jump aboard the next freight that was leaving.

With all the jostling of boxcars and shrieking of train whistles, it was plain a freight was about to go. Our gang shifted out of the bushes, ready to leap aboard, when suddenly two automobiles rushed up and blocked the way. Huddled together, we stood silently as men carrying clubs leaped out of the cars. A tall heavyset man stepped toward us, flashing a sheriff's badge.

"You kids are all under arrest! But don't be scared. We're not gonna hurt you unless you ask for it. Just behave and do as you're told."

I was scared stiff. Arrested! What flashed through my mind was what would Ma and Pa think! How did I ever get into this mess!

A couple of the youngest kids began to whimper, but

acting like their mom, Marge pulled them to her side. The sheriff moved closer to us. "We ain't gonna throw you in jail for long—if you just behave. Only one night and then you're outta here. Too many folks complaining about begging at their doors. Tomorrow morning you can hop the freight that leaves at eight. Meanwhile, we'll see that you get some supper, a warm bed, breakfast, and then you'll be on your way."

What could we say? Even Bernie kept his mouth shut. About six men left their cars to join the sheriff marching us to the town jail. Luckily, it wasn't far off. People on their porches or in front of stores stared at us. I felt they were more than used to bums. No one looked upset.

The jail was an old one-story cement-and-brick building. The sheriff's quarters were at one end, and the cells at the other. We were split into three groups—the girls put in one cell, and the rest of us in two others. A wooden bench lined three sides of my cell. No chair, no bed. I sat down, but some of the other guys just leaned against the cold wall.

Sometime later the sheriff came by and announced supper would be ready in fifteen minutes. But first, deputies would frisk us to see if anyone had knives or razors or guns. No one did. "And if you got money," he added, "I'll take it and return it in the morning." My fiver was long gone.

"There's a one-seater toilet in the corridor," he added. "If you need it, let us know."

Not much of a wait before the sheriff's wife and her helper came along, pulling our meal on two small carts. Through the space between the cell bars she handed each of us a pie tin with the promised supper. A cup of tomatoes, squeezed juice, a boiled potato, now cold, a slice of sugary bread. And then after serving all of us in the three cells, back she came with tin cups of water.

Hardly a square meal. But no one had the energy—or nerve—to complain. There was small chatter now and then in the cells, with long silences in between.

"What a nice warm bed," said Bernie, patting the wooden bench in our small cell. There wasn't room for all on the bench. The rest of us lay in our raggedy clothes on the cement floor. No blankets. I rolled on my side, using my arm as a pillow.

Who slept? How many hours, if any?

Morning arrived at last. The sheriff's deputy came to our cells around six, handing out washbasins, a small cake of hard soap, clumps of newspaper to use as towels. Then breakfast: a bowl of oatmeal with milk and sugar, a pair of fried eggs with a strip of bacon, two pieces of buttered toast, a dish of prunes, and coffee. A feast!

With train time at eight, the sheriff and his deputies arrived to walk us through town—and to our amazement, straight into a boxcar on the siding. "Okay now!"

he said. "All aboard the bums' special! Just remember, this town don't wanna see you ever again! Not ever!"

The sun was high enough to warm the air, even inside our boxcar. Several of the gang plunked themselves down with their backs against the wall, trying to make up for the previous night's broken sleep. Marge placed herself beside me.

"Joey, I never got a chance to thank you for getting that jerk Bernie off my back. He's one of those guys thinks every girl is a pushover. Well, I'm not! And he better know it now!"

"That's okay, Marge. I'm glad I could help. But tell me, where you from? And how come you're on the bum?"

"My dad was badly hurt working in a steel mill. No insurance—he didn't get a dime. The company kept him on three years, till the hard times came. Never could get a job after that. Mom got night work—you know, cleaning up? In a department store. But it was too much for her. She collapsed one night. They found her the next morning, on the floor. Rushed her to the hospital, but a day later she was gone. . . .

"My dad, he tried to keep a home for us three kids. But how could he with no job? I dropped out of school and hunted everywhere for work. But nobody wanted me. Our church placed my kid sisters in a home, my aunt took in my dad. And me, I just scrammed."

Made me think of Kate—could this ever happen to her?

The freight lumbered on, endlessly, it seemed, because I had lost all sense of time, with no day punctuated by events, either routine or extraordinary. I dozed off finally, only to dream of home, reliving the routine of long ago. Suddenly, I realized I'd not let anyone know where I was—Kate, Ma, Pa, Grandpa, Newt—the people who meant so much to me.

Just then the train banged to a stop, and we all gathered at the boxcar door. A yardman opened it, stepped aside, and let us leap off one by one.

"Where are we? What's the name of this dump?"

"You're in a rail yard," the man said, "just outside Chicago."

"Is there a church nearby?" I asked.

"Yeah, there is. And with a mission, too. So you guys can maybe get some chow. Even a bed."

It was less than two miles off. "Anyone going there?" I asked.

No one, it seemed, wanted to. They'd rather try to hitch a ride into the big city. Even walk it. But me, I felt I had to talk to someone back home, to let them know I was still here, still breathing, still hoping. For what, I didn't know.

21

Well, I found my way to the church mission. An old lady appeared to be in charge, and when I told her how long I'd been away from home, about the Bonus March, and how I'd been there with my father, she said she'd heard about it and seen it in the news-reels, and couldn't get over how mean that man Hoover was.

"But what can I do for you?"

I said my folks didn't know where I was and could I use the phone to call collect?

"Of course you can, son. It's here in my office, to the right."

I hesitated at her desk. Who to call? I feared bad news might be waiting for me. I'd better try Kate first. So I gave the operator her number. After the second ring, Kate's voice came through. When the operator spoke my name, Kate screamed, "Joey! Joey! Where are you? Are you all right?"

I hurried through what had happened to me in the weeks I'd been gone, but I never said why I'd run off.

Once, when I paused for breath, Kate murmured, "Joey, I love you."

I learned that Pa and Newt had gone to the authorities in Washington to find out where Hank's body had been taken. It was in the newspaper. But no one would admit Hank had been killed. Apparently, someone higher up had imposed silence. It was as though Hank had never existed.

When Pa and Newt returned home, Ma learned of her runaway son. I feared how she might have reacted. But Kate said she'd gone to see my mother and found her taking my flight stoically. "He'll come back. He will, he will, I know it," she had kept on saying.

As for Newt, Kate had seen him, too. He'd been close to cracking up at Hank's death. This, on top of the loss of his wife and younger child. . . . But somehow he had to go on living, had to go back to work. And he'd taken on another young guy. Guessing what was on Kate's mind, he'd told her the new man understood it was temporary, till I'd return.

"But Kate, Kate, this call must be costing you a fortune!"

"No matter, Joey. I still have my job. And it may seem hard to believe, but so does my dad! A new job, a better job! Somehow he met a man living in that apartment house where he worked. Turned out to be the managing editor of the Chicago *Daily News*. And when he heard Dad's name, he instantly recognized it. He said, 'You're the man who wrote that super piece in *Harper's*! About the devastated mill towns of New England.'"

And, Kate continued, a week later the man had hired her father to do what was called "investigative reporting"—on the widespread corruption in both the city and state governments in Illinois.

I was delighted to hear good news at last. But then Kate added that Mr. Williams wanted his family to move to Chicago to join him. Not right away; no, he felt he'd better wait a few months to make sure the newspaper would like his reporting and keep him on. His pay was pretty good, and he was able to send them enough to get by in the meantime.

I didn't tell Kate I felt responsible for Hank's death. I could hardly voice it even to myself. In these weeks on the bum I'd thought of it often, seen it happening again and again. . . . "I'll come home soon," I promised her. "But not just now. I need a little more time. Call it growing-up time, or whatever. And can I ask you to tell my folks I'm okay? That I'll write them soon."

Before we hung up, Kate gave me her dad's phone number and address. "Call him—he always liked you, Joey. He's asked me more than once what you were up to. I'm sure he'll be glad to hear from you. And Joey, you must need money! Look, I'll wire you ten dollars. You go to the nearest Western Union office tomorrow, and they'll have it for you."

That made me feel funny, but I sure could use it.

I decided to call her dad. And right away, before I lost my nerve. I begged the mission lady to let me make just one more call. She hesitated, then said, "But make it quick!"

Luckily, Mr. Williams was at home, and he greeted me warmly. When I told him I was in Chicago, he asked me to come see him and repeated the address Kate had given me. "I'll be working out of town the next couple of days. How about Thursday? Come at seven, and we'll have something for supper."

Walking back to our hangout, I realized I needed to look at least halfway decent to see Kate's dad. I decided to ask Marge for help. The girls in our gang often did this for the guys—washing clothes, sewing on buttons, patching pants, cutting hair. I told her why I needed help, and she began right away to neaten my clothes, even scissoring my shaggy mop so I didn't look too bad.

The next morning I found out where the nearest Western Union was, and sure enough, when I told them my name, they handed me ten singles—more money than I'd seen since Lord knows when.

Those two days waiting for my visit with Kate's dad seemed to go on forever. But finally I found myself at the entry to his apartment house. Big—ten stories high! The doorman looked suspiciously at me in my dungarees and rain jacket, but when he called Mr. Williams, he was told to let me go up.

The apartment was on the second floor rear. When he answered the doorbell and saw me, Mr. Williams shook my hand warmly and put an arm over my shoulder as he let me in. It was what they call a studio apartment—just one small room with a sleeping couch, a kitchenette in one corner, and next to it a small dining table. A couple of scatter rugs lay on the floor.

I knew he'd want to know where his daughter's boyfriend had been all this time. While he asked me questions, he fixed two platters of hamburgers and French fries, a pot of coffee, and some rolls, then announced, "Apple pie with chocolate ice cream will follow!"

I told him what I'd told Kate, trying to make it short. He was intensely interested in my account of the hobo life I'd been living and kept asking for more details. He mentioned that his paper had run stories about the flophouses in Chicago, the breadlines, and the Hoovervilles in the vacant lots and parks.

"But all that was from the outside," he said. "Not by people who themselves were the victims of this awful Depression the country's going through."

We sat there quietly for a while, with me slowly enjoying that delectable dessert. Then he said, "Joey, I've got an idea. You've been living with boys and girls who should be in school and at home. Instead, they're wandering the country on freight trains and living in hobo jungles. You know their struggle to feed and clothe themselves. You know what it is to be hungry and cold, to beg for a crust or for a dime, or for a warm place to sleep. I believe you've got a story to tell, a nightmare to reveal. . . . Why don't you write it up?"

His excitement stunned me. Write it up? Me? Who'd read it? "Who'd care about a gang of kids on the bum?" I asked.

"Almost anyone would," he said. "Look, we're in the third year of this damn Depression. Statistics pile high about how awful it's been. But little has been said or done about the children whose lives have been shattered—the boys and girls you've been living with. You know it from the inside. What you could report is news, news the government especially needs to know—and to do something about."

I sure was excited by the idea. But me? Barely seventeen, trying to do this? What made him think I could pull it off?

"You can do it, Joey, you can, I know you can. Whenever Kate brought home the school magazine, I'd read your pieces, and I always liked them."

"All right," I said. "But if I did try what you suggest, who'd print it?"

"Leave that to me. If it comes out good, I'll take it to our editor. And if he agrees with me . . . you're in print."

Well, it was a proposal I couldn't say no to. We

worked out how I'd tackle it. Mr. Williams said I should stay with him for as long as it took, sleeping on a folding cot he had. Each day I'd write my draft in longhand. He'd read and edit the manuscript at night. Next day he'd have a woman in the office secretarial pool type it up. "Just one caution, Joey. Be sure you don't use the real names of the people you describe. We've got to protect their privacy."

After breakfast the next morning (hot cereal, ham and eggs, rolls, coffee—I felt like I was being fattened up for a sacrifice!) I went back to my gang to pick up the few things I had left there. And to tell them a man was giving me some work, and I might be gone a few days or even a week. I didn't tell them what that work would be. I'd feel awful if my stuff was lousy and the paper didn't run it.

When I returned to Mr. Williams's place around noon, the doorman handed me the apartment key. "I understand you'll be staying on for several days," he said. "Just be sure you lock up anytime you go out. Been some robberies around here lately."

As I entered the apartment, I saw a thick 8½ X 11 notebook on the table, with a fountain pen next to it. I sat down, picked up the pen, opened the notebook to the first page, and stared blankly at it. Scared to start? Minutes passed and I couldn't get going. I got up and paced the room. Back and forth, back and forth. No words, no sentences, no thoughts. Then I lay down on the couch and let my mind float. I don't know how much time had passed when thoughts began to drift into my head.

Find your way to a starting point. Don't think about the weeks with the gang as a whole, start with just one kid you got to know. What did you learn from him, his family life, his reasons for leaving home, his first days on the move, how this life changed his feelings, his ideas. And how at some point he melted into the gang. Or ran away from it.

It was hours before I put pen to paper and managed to scrawl the first sentences. I chose Bernie to start with. Because I detested him? Distrusted him? Wanted to figure him out?

When Mr. Williams came home, he asked how it was going.

"Slowly," I said, "very slowly."

"Don't worry, that's often the case. But once you feel the swing of it, the rhythm will move you along."

There wasn't enough down on paper for him to begin editing. "We'll wait a while," he said, "till you're in full swing."

That night I phoned home—the first direct call in quite a while. Ma answered. Her voice shot way up when she heard me. I expected I'd get hell, but not at all. She was only glad to hear I was well and working with Mr. Williams. And she had big news for me.

"Joey, you've got mail from that New College you

applied to! I opened it, and they said not only are you accepted but they're giving you a full year's scholarship. Imagine! Four hundred dollars! And to cover your dormitory room and your meals, you'll have a job serving breakfast every morning in the college dining hall!"

She told me that New College would open a bit later than expected—not until late September. So I had time to work with Mr. Williams till we were finished. Each night after supper he'd go over my manuscript pages. He'd underline a word or a phrase he wanted me to think about and scribble notes here and there in the margin. He had me cut out repetition, too many adjectives or adverbs, and passages so vaguely worded that the idea was lost.

Be definite, he told me; use specific, concrete language. Sometimes I thought his voice echoed Aggie Larkin's. She, too, would say, Don't worry about style. Let it come naturally.

It took me five days to do it. I'd said all I had to say. On the table was a stack of neatly typed pages. Mr. Williams had me read them carefully to see if I was ready for his editor's judgment. "You look scared," he said. "Not to worry! You won't be executed!"

I felt that I had to phone Kate. Turned out she knew of my great break at New College. Aggie Larkin had told her. "And I have news for you! I'll be starting college, too. At Radcliffe. Now that Dad's got a steady job, he's borrowing the four hundred dollars for tuition. And maybe I'll earn a scholarship if my grades are good enough. Dad urged me not to tell you till you knew whether you'd be going to college. Didn't want to upset you."

I was happy for her. But how often could we be together if she was in another city? She reassured me. We'd not be too far apart, and bus rides were cheap.

I could hardly wait to return home. "Only a day or two more," Mr. Williams said. "Tomorrow morning I'll give the piece to the editor. He knows you've been working on it. He makes quick decisions. In this business you have to. I should know in a few hours. I'll phone you right away."

That was a sleepless night. My writing—was it worth anything? Was Mr. Williams just trying to make me feel good? Then I told myself, Forget it, you never thought you'd be a writer. There are lots of other ways to make a living.

I guess I fell asleep at last.

At three in the afternoon the next day the phone rang. It was Kate's dad. "Joey? You're in! You made it! The boss thinks the piece is so good, he's going to start it on page one. And he's asked me to write an editorial tied to it. He thinks we should urge Congress to pass legislation setting up programs to help young people in need, whether in school or out. Maybe some sort of financial subsidy for students. A work-and-study plan that would help young people stay in school till they graduate. And if they're eighteen or so and in need of a job, a federal program that would pay them to work in a conservation program—reforestation, road construction, flood control—projects like that."

It sounded great to me. But then, if I'd learned anything from the history we'd studied, it would take a lot of organized political pressure to get the government to move.

That night when Mr. Williams came in from work, he said we had to celebrate. So he took me out for dinner. An elegant French restaurant, with linen tablecloths, silverware, four courses, and a rich dessert. I couldn't thank him enough for all he'd done for me. When we got home and I was about to tuck into my cot, I reached out and hugged him.

22

It was a long bus ride from Illinois to Massachusetts. Kate's dad had handed me the newspaper's payment for my piece—in cash, twenty dollars!—but I didn't want to spend any of it on a train ticket. When I reached our three-decker after endless hours on the road, I raced up the stairs, shoved open the back door with a bang, and yelled, "Folks! Here I am!" They were all there, Ma and Pa and Grandpa, sitting at the kitchen table, sipping tea. It was the warmest welcome—hugs and kisses and how much they'd missed me. In spite of all my craziness . . . No one said a word bawling me out over the long absence and the long silence. How could they, when I showed them that Chicago newspaper with my piece—and my name!—right there on page 1.

That night, when Grandpa and I were in our beds, I heard him quietly crooning a Yiddish folk tune.

"A lullaby, Grandpa, to make me sleep?"

He laughed. "A big boy needs that?"

"No, but it helps."

"Tell me, Joey—something I don't understand. None of us. We've talked about it so many times since you ran away. Why did you do it? You must have been terribly upset by Hank's death. But still . . ."

We lay there silently for a while. Then Grandpa went on: "Did you feel guilty about that boy's death? That you had done something wrong? Something maybe you were ashamed of?"

How could he know the pain, the horror of those moments? It swept over me again. I couldn't answer him.

Grandpa slid out of his bed and sat down on the edge of mine. He put his warm palm on my cheek, wet with tears.

"Tell me, Joey. It can be a secret between us."

Slowly I began to whisper, to tell what had happened that night, how the soldiers had rushed down on us, burning, destroying, how one of them had reached us with bayonet thrusting, and how I'd run away, too scared to stand my ground, to help Hank defend himself—and then turned to find Hank dying at my feet.

"Joey boy, you can't blame yourself for that. People act by instinct at such terrible times. You remember what I told you how your grandma—the grandma you never knew—lost her life?"

"Yes, Grandpa, the pogrom."

"That day . . . how can I tell you? . . . A drunken mob rushed into our neighborhood. They broke into shops, into homes, they smashed furniture, stole everything in sight, beat anyone in their way. Soon they were killing people even in their homes. A mob caught Rose and me running to hide somewhere, anywhere, and when they came closer and closer, I was almost crazy with fear, and I ran into an alley hoping they'd miss us. I thought Rose was running right behind me, but she wasn't. I didn't stop to make sure. . . . Suddenly, I realized I was running alone, with no one behind me. I was sick. I ran back, and there at the turnoff was my Rose, lying on the street—in a pool of blood." His voice choked up and tears flooded down.

"Joey, Joey, I blamed myself for her death for years, years. But now I see it was all part of a madness, the mob, the victims, a blind, unreasoning thing that will seize anyone in such an awful moment.

"Joey, it wasn't your fault. It wasn't! I know it."

I fell asleep, at peace with myself, knowing now that though I'd failed Hank, it wasn't out of cowardice.

I slept late, real late for the first time in a long while. When I got up, Pa had already gone off to his early job at the Sterling cafeterias. But he'd left fifteen dollars on the breakfast table.

"For you," Ma said. "Ever since we knew for sure you'd be going to college, we all began pinching pennies even harder so you could buy a new suit at Ware Pratt. First time a Singer gets to college, he can't shame the family looking like a rag doll!"

165

With the money left over from what the Chicago paper paid me, I'd be able to buy decent shoes, a new shirt, and a tie, too. I had but two days to go before registering at New College. I couldn't see Kate. She'd begun classes at Radcliffe. But Ma had a letter Kate had asked her to hold for me. On the back of the envelope she'd printed HUGS AND KISSES! Inside, she told me she'd read my Chicago article again and again, and knew for sure that I'd be a writer. "Hemingway, watch out! Faulkner, move over!" she scrawled at the bottom of her loving message. "Hang on till Christmas," she closed, "and we'll have the greatest homecoming party ever."

She promised to write once a week and knew I'd do the same.

I had just one other thing to do before leaving home. I stayed up very late that night and walked out to Hymie Ruch's store around the time I knew Newt would stop by there. A few minutes later the milk truck arrived, and Newt jumped out. We looked at each other silently for a moment. Then I reached into my pocket and gave him that snapshot of Hank and me, laughing at how clever we were. He took it and stared at it a long time, and then we moved and held each other in a long embrace. "My son, my son," he whispered.

HISTORICAL NOTE

Only a few months after the stock market collapsed in the fall of 1929, the number of unemployed Americans jumped from fewer than half a million to more than four million. At first, many people believed that the economy would soon recover. But it slid downward, faster and faster. By 1932 more than twelve million people were out of work. Breadlines and soup kitchens were seen in every city. And about a million desperate people, many of them young and hopeless, wandered everywhere, hitching rides, hopping freight trains, tramping city streets and country roads.

Unemployment became a way of life, and out of it developed a new style of housing: shantytowns, made of tin cans and packing boxes, that sprang up in vacant lots, in parks, along the river's edge.

Many of the unemployed, stunned by the crisis, turned inward, resigned to their fate or blaming themselves for their economic misfortune. But others joined unions and voted to tax themselves small sums to aid the jobless in their trades. Unemployed people formed local groups that appealed to farmers in their area to let them dig potatoes or pick fruit. In New York's Harlem and on Chicago's South Side, jazz musicians performed at "rent parties" for small sums that would pay overdue rent and prevent evictions.

What made the biggest headlines and won the greatest sympathy for the unemployed was the Bonus March of 1932—the true story that is at the heart of this novel. In 1924, Congress passed a bill promising each World War I veteran a cash bonus of about five hundred dollars—but it was not to be paid until 1945. With more and more veterans devastated by the worsening Depression, they began demanding that the government honor its pledge immediately. In the spring of 1932, more than twenty thousand veterans from all over the country converged on Washington, D.C., to press for action right *then*.

An uneasy President Herbert Hoover, fearing an insurrection, ordered federal troops to remove the Bonus Marchers from federal property after the police failed in their attempt to do so. Chief of Staff General Douglas MacArthur ordered an attack. Using tanks, tear gas, machine guns, and cavalry with fixed bayonets, the troops routed the demonstrators, leaving some veterans and two police officers dead.

Finally, in January 1936, Congress, over President Franklin D. Roosevelt's veto, passed a law providing for payment of the veterans' bonus.

Joey, Kate, Hank, their families, and the other characters in the novel are fictional. But what happens to them, what they go through, rises out of the history of those tough times.